ALISON DeCAMP

A Yearling Book

 Published in the United States by Yearling, an imprint of Random House Children's Books, a division of Penguin Random House LLC, New York.
Originally published in hardcover in the United States by Crown Books for Young Readers, New York, in 2015.

Yearling and the jumping horse design are registered trademarks of Penguin Random House LLC.

Visit us on the Web! randomhousekids.com

Educators and librarians, for a variety of teaching tools, visit us at RHTeachersLibrarians.com

The Library of Congress has cataloged the hardcover edition of this work as follows:
DeCamp, Alison.
My near-death adventures (99% true!) / Alison DeCamp. — First edition.
pages cm.
Summary: In 1895, eleven-year-old Stan decides to find his long-lost father in the logging camps of Michigan, documenting in his scrapbook his travels and encounters with troublesome relatives, his mother's suitors, lumberjacks, and more.
ISBN 978-0-385-39044-6 (trade) — ISBN 978-0-385-39046-0 (ebook)
[1. Adventure and adventurers—Fiction. 2. Missing persons—Fiction. 3. Logging—Fiction. 4. Family life—Michigan—Fiction. 5. Scrapbooks—Fiction. 6. Michigan—History—19th century—Fiction. 7. Humorous stories.] I. Title.
PZ7.1.D43My 2015 [Fic]—dc23 2014017792

ISBN 978-0-385-39047-7 (pbk.)

Printed in the United States of America
10 9 8 7 6 5 4 3 2
First Yearling Edition 2016

Random House Children's Books supports the First Amendment and celebrates the right to read.

To my own sweet mama

Conrad McAllister.

Only Conrad's uglier.

CHAPTER 1

Who you callin’ ugly?” Conrad McAllister asks. His breath could melt the snow right off the roof, and I can’t help pinching my nose.

“And now you sayin’ I stink?”

For the record, I did *not* say Conrad was ugly. I said he was “*plug* ugly,” and I whispered it to Lydia Mae.

People should not be punished for telling the truth. Mama always says, “The Lord does not bless a lie,” and it is not a lie that Conrad McAllister’s parents had to tie a pork chop to his neck when he was little so their dog would play with him.

“Um, Stan, that’s a lie.” Lydia Mae elbows me.

"Does he know we can hear him?" Conrad says to Lydia Mae.

She shrugs sheepishly.

Conrad returns his attention to me. "Well, what do you have to say for yourself? Huh?"

I think for a minute. What *do* I have to say for myself?

Lydia Mae straightens herself up. She's about even with my shoulder. "Anyway, Conrad, you've got the wrong person," she says bravely. "I'm the one who called you ugly."

I should not have a girl taking my licks for me. I should step in and take responsibility for my actions. I should. But I might not.

"Again," Conrad says, "we can hear you, you lily-livered milksop." He takes a step closer, his fists clenched.

"Run, Stan! Run!" Lydia Mae yells. She jumps on Conrad's back, yanking the cap over his eyes while he hops around like a dog with fleas, and I take off toward my house, the soles of my boots flip-flopping through the snow.

Mama always says I'm about as focused as a swarm of drunken bees, but during this run home, I *am* focused. I'm focused on staying alive as I make a list in my head of how to avoid Conrad for the rest of my life, or at least until he's finally in jail. But as soon as I slam the door of the apartment house and am safely inside, I spy it, and immediately Conrad McAllister is a distant memory.

An envelope. I've seen it before. And even though my imminent death by Conrad McAllister's ham-hock fists seems more important, he doesn't really scare me. He'll forget this

little incident by the next time we meet. Also, as has been proven again and again, I can outrun him.

But the envelope seems suspicious, even for someone who doesn't have what Mama claims is an "overactive imagination," because little things have been happening since it showed up. For one, Mama seems to stare off into space a lot. Also, her fingers don't stop tapping, and I've had to make most of my own meals since she's been working more than ever, meals that have not been of the best quality due to the poor choice of food I have to work with. Leftover meat and stale bread from the general store where Mama tends the counter do not lead to much but a lot of dry salt-pork sandwiches.

So when I see that envelope on the kitchen counter, it's as hard to ignore as my empty stomach at three o'clock in the afternoon. And that reminds me . . .

It's three o'clock in the afternoon.

And I'm so hungry I could eat everything on a pig but the oink.

I stuff a hunk of bread in my mouth instead and look at the envelope more closely, now that I know it's not as innocent as it looks.

To tell God's honest truth (which, of course, is the only kind of truth I ever tell), the first time I saw the envelope, I didn't think much of it. Heck, it was just an envelope; it didn't look like it would turn my life all topsy-turvy. I picked it up, saw the sharp slit across the top and the empty space inside, and set it back on the table. Then I got on with some very important business.

Planning for my twelfth birthday.

I had a fresh catalog and a blank page in my Scrapbook. Plus some scissors I borrowed in the not-asking kind of way from my mama's bedside table.

Just to be clear, the scissors are mine. They were only briefly put somewhere else because of the time my cousin Geri cut holes in the curtains and blamed it on me. To be fair, however, those curtains were so ugly they made onions cry.

When I opened the catalog, I found a harmonica, a saddle, some firearms, and a trick bank—just the simple necessities of any self-respecting almost-twelve-year-old boy.

And I didn't think anything more about the envelope.

Not that day, anyway.

Because Mama came peering over my shoulder and asked me what I was doing, and next thing I knew, she had snuggled up to me like butter on warm toast.

I told her about the money we would save with a tricky kind of bank. It would be smart to give me one for my birthday, even though it costs a dollar twenty-five, enough money to feed us for a week.

"It doesn't cost anything to look and very little to wish," Mama said as she snipped the picture from the Montgomery Ward catalog. "Also, we have lots of time for hoping—your birthday is almost a whole year away."

"Practically around the corner," I replied, and Mama smiled.

I remember like it was yesterday, because ever since that envelope arrived, Mama's smile has been as scarce as peaches in January, and her eyebrows have been knitted together so often the crease in between looks carved in stone.

A week later, I found the envelope crumpled on the table, which wouldn't seem suspicious in anyone else's house, I'm sure. But in our house, nothing is crumpled. Mama either irons it, throws it away, or sends it to its room to put on some less wrinkly pants. She attacks messes like her very soul depends on it. If cleanliness is next to Godliness, Mama could be God's Siamese twin.

Let's do something fun!
No! We need to work! And then clean!
Don't you EVER stop cleaning?
Let's play some fun music! And then we'll clean!
Won't you ever stop cleaning?
When we're done, let's get the broom and sweep up the sawdust.
It's your turn to clean.
That's great! I LOVE cleaning!
Stop fidgeting!
But all the guts and feathers! It's so messy!
This is getting ridiculous.
You stay here and catch some dinner. I need to clean the kitchen. It's a mess!
First one back gets to clean the parlor!
Can't this horse go any faster? I have to get home and clean!
"CHANG" AND "ENG"
THE WORLD RENOWNED UNITED
SIAMESE TWINS.

"We don't have much," she says, "but we take care of what we have."

Mama has the horrible habit of picking up perfectly fine paper and calling it garbage, a habit that's only gotten worse in the last couple of weeks. If she picks up something once, it's a warning, and twice it's in the trash, which is why my very important discoveries are immediately pasted in my Scrapbook. And why I'm sometimes found rescuing things from the garbage. And also why the crumpled-up envelope was so strange just sitting there on the kitchen table.

I'm not the type of fellow who jumps to conclusions, so although the situation seemed as strange as a dog wearing glasses, I most definitely did not overreact when I spied it for the second time.

I am not known to overreact. Also, I'm pretty sure no one even heard me scream.

The third time I saw it, however, was cause for genuine panic. It was eight days ago, and the envelope was firmly clenched in the claws of a scary old woman.

17. Dr. Yellow Collie. An Earnest Student.

CHAPTER 2

The old woman grabbed the envelope off the counter, marched into Mama's room, and slammed the door behind her. Which was rude, if you ask me, but if you ask the old lady, who insists I call her Granny, she would say it's none of my business. In fact, that's exactly what she said when I asked her. "Stanley Arthur Slater, that is none of your business."

To which I replied, "Hogwash!" A saying, you will be surprised to find out, that has nothing to do with washing a hog, but rather means "You don't know what you're talking about, woman!"

I overheard a little of the conversation with Mama be-

cause Granny talks very loudly and maybe also because my ear was pressed so hard against the door it felt like I had a keyhole in my left cheek. I had tried looking through the keyhole, but all I could see was Granny's backside, so you can understand why that angle didn't work.

The problem was I couldn't hear much except "fresh start" and "money" and "camp" and "worthless Arthur Slater" and something about a pickle, but don't quote me on that.

Hearing the words "Arthur Slater" made me feel as confused as a moth in a room full of candles, because it just so happens that's two-thirds of my name right there. It also just so happens to be the name of my dearly departed father, and most bewildering of all: Worthless?

Now the envelope lies abandoned on the kitchen counter, apparently dropped or forgotten. It's addressed to Mama, and the words "Colorado, Texas" curl around the stamp like a dog chasing its tail. The date, DEC 14, 1894, tattoos half of Mr. George Washington's face. Personally, I think it is nothing short of disrespectful to tattoo Mr. Honest George, our forefather who chopped down his very own log cabin and was the first to sign the Declaration of Dependence.

I am a whiz at history, I don't mind saying.

I nab the envelope, not like I'm *stealing* it, more as if I am *saving* it. It seems like it has some connection to my father, and I don't have anything that's connected to my father except for my handsome looks and a slightly lazy eye; Granny says anything that lazy had to have come from my dad. Plus, that envelope has been hanging around so long now I feel like it's a family member, the kind of family member who brings bad news and spits out worse breath. The kind of family member who comes and never leaves.

"Who never leaves?" Granny barks as she grumps into the room. I stuff the envelope in my pocket and do my best impression of someone innocent.

I am a whiz at looking innocent, I don't mind saying.

Unfortunately, I'm not a whiz at keeping thoughts tucked firmly between my ears. Sometimes those thoughts come straight out my mouth. Fortunately, I have become something of an expert at covering up this slight flaw in my character.

"I repeat, 'Who never leaves?'" Granny scowls.

"Um, what's that, Granny? What I said was, 'Mark Twain is rumored to have fleas.'"

"What on earth can you mean?" Granny huffs as if I'm taking the very name of the Lord in vain. "Mr. Mark Twain most certainly does *not* have fleas!"

Granny loves Mark Twain. She talked to him once in a train station in Chicago and swears she inspired him to write *Huck Finn*. More likely, she trapped him in a corner of the men's room, talked his ear off, and inspired the character of Miss Watson, the miserable woman who owns Jim as a slave.

"Mr. Twain and I had a bond," she says dreamily. I'm 103.4 percent certain the only bond Granny has is with a loup-garou, otherwise known as a French werewolf.

And a French werewolf is the worst kind of all, not just because of its strange accent. I'd know because my friend Lydia Mae loves to tell me stories about them when there's a full moon. Plus, I have a picture of one on page 12 of my Scrapbook.

"Are you listening, young man?" Granny swings her head around like she's looking for something. "Have you seen an envelope lying anywhere?"

"Uh, no," I reply like it's the dumbest question I've heard this week. It's actually not. Tuesday at school, Conrad McAllister asked our teacher, Mrs. Huggins, why feet smell and noses run. *That* is the dumbest question I've heard this week and completely deserving of the dunce cap Mrs. Huggins placed firmly on Conrad's head.

Granny has a puzzled look on her

face, so I take this opportunity to ask the question that has been dogging me forever. Or at least since 11:35. "Why were you talking about my dearly departed father, Granny? And why is he worthless?"

Now, Granny looks at me like marbles are settling in her brain. "What are you talking about? What 'dearly departed father'?"

Where has this woman been? "The dearly departed father who is never around because he's dead," I explain, a tiny bit of exasperation edging into my voice. "You don't remember him? You knew him better than I ever did!"

"Stan, what makes you think your father has, um, how can I say this delicately? Hmmm. Bought the farm?"

"I don't think he bought a farm, Granny," I explain patiently. "We are not a family of farmers."

Granny pats her hair distractedly, tucking a stray curl behind her ear and then smoothing her apron. She takes a deep breath. "No, Stan. What I mean is, why are you under the impression your father has died?"

"Um, well, because every time in my whole life I've ever brought up the subject of my father, you say he's dead to you. At Thanksgiving I overheard you tell Uncle Carl that Arthur dug himself a grave and was a deadbeat. And every time I've asked Mama to tell me about my father, she just says to pray for his soul. So obviously he's no longer with us. In the living sense, I mean."

Granny looks down at me like I'm slightly blurry and gives her head a brief shake. "It is true your father is no longer with us," she says, staring me right in the peepers. "But it's not because he's dead."

Suddenly my stomach feels just like the time Conrad McAllister slugged me in the gut when I told him he'd never be the man his mother is.

In my defense, his mother has a mustache.

All the air rushes from me, and my head feels too big for my hat. What did Granny just say? He's not dead? Wait a minute! How can this be? How could my father be alive but never try to get ahold of Mama or me? "He's alive?" I ask Granny, my voice as pitchy as a clarinet in the Independence Day parade.

Granny looks past me and slowly answers, "Yes, that's what is often meant by 'not dead.' Your long-lost father is definitely alive."

"He's lost?" I ask. This would explain why he has never been around. My entire life my father has been a hazy dream, appearing like a shadow in the night when I'm alone in my room. Or he's been the cowlick on top of my head, the stubborn hair Mama always tries so hard to smooth down, the hair Mama says I got from my father—the father I thought was too dearly departed to teach me to toss a baseball on summer Sunday afternoons. The very same father I needed to show me how to put a worm on a hook and tell me not to stand up in a boat.

And of all the luck, just as I hear my father is alive, lo and behold, he's lost.

"We need to find him!" I exclaim. "And save him!"

"Oh, I'm pretty sure there's no saving him," Granny says under her breath. "Also, aside from a brief letter from Texas, we have no idea where he is."

"But he wrote to us!" I grasp on to this fact as if I'm drowning and someone has just thrown me a life jacket. "He must have said something about me. Where does he want us to meet him?"

"Stan, the letter he sent was a matter between adults," Granny says, her voice hard, her eyes a steely gray.

FIG. 11.—CORK JACKET AND LIFE-BUOY.

"But did he say he would visit us? Is he coming here, or are we meeting him in Texas? When did you see him?" I pepper Granny with questions.

Granny rubs her temple like it hurts. "I truly don't think I'd recognize your father if he walked in the front door, it's been so long since I've laid eyes on that sorry excuse for a man. And he honestly could be anywhere—Texas last week, California next week.

The North Pole. The circus. Anywhere." I stare at her as she blathers on. "He could have a different name now, for all I know. He could call himself Chicken McPhee and herd cattle out on the range. And a man like Arthur Slater usually does not want to be found."

Of course he wants to be found! Especially when he could pass all his secrets on to his son. Like how to find gold and herd cattle.

Granny's eyes soften, which is not a look I'm familiar with. "Your father is the type of man who . . ." She pauses to think. "Doesn't like to be tied down."

"Of course not! Who wants to be tied down, Granny? Conrad McAllister tied me down to the tree next to the schoolhouse once. Believe me, it is no fun. I couldn't move my arms, and when it started to rain, everyone ran inside and I got soaking wet." I completely understand why my father would not want to be tied down.

Granny lifts my chin so my eyes meet hers. "You'll better understand when you're a man," she says, and hurries from the room.

But I don't have time to wait to become a man, not now that I know my father's out there somewhere, lost and just waiting to be found.

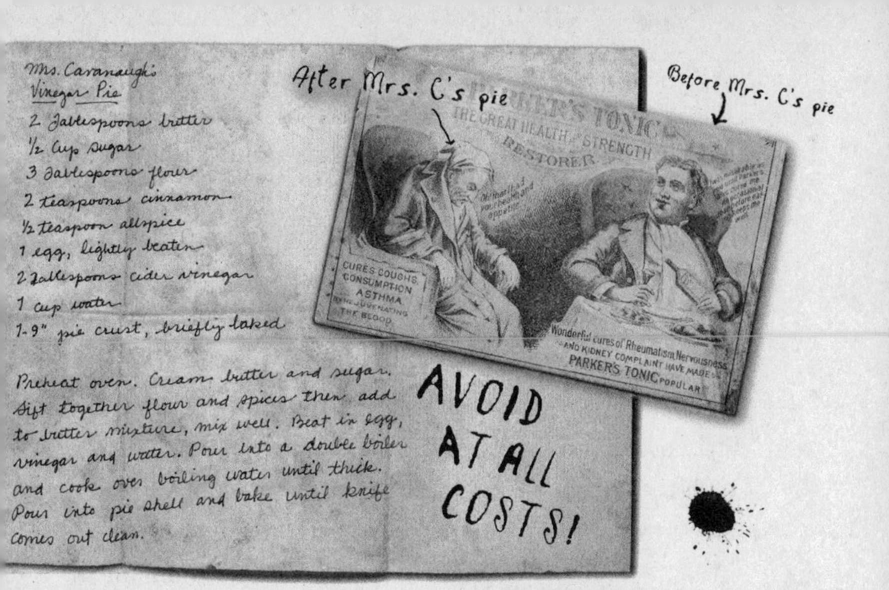

CHAPTER 3

I can always tell when Mrs. Cavanaugh raps on the door; it's a knock as demanding as the sneeze you try to hold back in church. I open the door slightly, only to spy a pile of letters in one hand and another dreadful vinegar pie in the other. I sure hope she doesn't notice the two partially eaten ones still sitting on the stove, and I cringe at the thought of Mama making me eat more of that pie. "We are not in the position to waste good food," she says. I want to point out that vinegar pie is the opposite of good food, but I don't think it will help the situation. Plus, lately she hasn't really been paying close attention to whether I've been cleaning my plate. Actually, lately she hasn't really been paying attention to much. She even shooed me out of the house yesterday to go play with "that nice Conrad McAllister," which made Lydia Mae and me laugh so hard I almost thought it was funny.

Reminder: there's nothing funny about Conrad McAllister.

"I've brought your mail and a nice pie for your dinner," Mrs. Cavanaugh says, barging in. Granny says Mrs. Cavanaugh is "big-boned" and has "ears like an elephant and a memory to match." She also claims her "tongue wags more than a dog's tail in a room full of bones." I'm not quite sure what she means, but I'm pretty sure it's not nice.

Mrs. Cavanaugh thrusts the pie at me and fans herself with our mail. Her neck cranes around, the ridiculous flower on her hat bouncing about like her eyes, darting from the frayed rug at our feet to the hall mirror to the parlor. I set the pie on the table and reach for the letters.

Some letters, I have learned, may hold secrets. Important secrets, say, about a certain someone's long-lost father.

I am a whiz at secrets, I don't mind saying. Although, I will admit, I might not be such a whiz at *keeping* secrets.

Mrs. Cavanaugh clutches the mail to her chest. "Stan," she says seriously, looking over the rims of her spectacles, "that might be the most honest thing you've ever said. We all know keeping your mouth shut is not your specialty."

I get ready to argue, but I am pretty sure this difficult human will only insist on bringing up the time I may or may not have mentioned to Conrad McAllister that Mrs. Cavanaugh's rather enormous pink bloomers were hanging on the line. The very same Conrad McAllister who may or may not have alerted all the neighborhood kids to witness these large underdrawers. And the exact same Conrad McAllister who taught the whole neighborhood to chant:

Mrs. C. wears bloomers so giant,
Even David couldn't beat this Goliath.
They're so big and so pink
And they probably stink.
I think it is time for a diet.

Mrs. Cavanaugh is not known for her sense of humor, but what can I say? It's a rough neighborhood.

"What do you have there?" she asks, leaning toward the old envelope I've absentmindedly pulled from my pocket. It appears to be like a piece of steel and she is a magnet—when I wave the envelope around, her head bobbles with it. I quickly tuck it away.

"Oh, nothing," I answer casually.

"Did I notice that your grandmother arrived a week

ago? I was wondering why. I like to keep a watchful eye on my neighbors, you know. Especially when there's no man around. And lately I can't help noticing you seem to be left unsupervised more than is appropriate." She pinches her lips together. "I haven't seen your grandma Cora since old Percy Marvin's funeral. Was that two years ago?"

"Well," I respond, "Granny was just in town at Thanksgiving—don't know how you missed her. And I'm sorry to say, but I'm not all too familiar with this Percy Marvin fellow, Mrs. Cavanaugh, although he sounds quite, um, dead-ish." I have been taught to be respectful of the dearly departed, seeing as my father was one of them until recently. "And, yes, ma'am, we have the pleasure of another visit from Granny," I add, thinking that a visit from Granny is about as pleasurable as a visit from the plague doctor.

"And who was the man driving the wagon that dropped off your grandmother?" Mrs. Cavanaugh's eyes widen.

I think for a minute. "Do you mean Uncle Carl . . . ?"

Her interest immediately fades. "Oh, by the way, here's your mail." She stretches an arm toward me, but right before I can snatch up the letters, she pulls back and examines the one on top. "Hmmm. One from Omaha? Who could be from

Omaha?" Her eyes sparkle dangerously. "Isn't your father from around there?"

"I . . . I don't know," I say cautiously. Is my father from Omaha? And if I act dumb, will Mrs. Cavanaugh tell me more about him?

She tut-tuts. "He certainly was a ne'er-do-well, that man. I forgot he skipped town right before you were born. After spending his entire winter's earnings at the saloon, that is."

I glare at her. The old windbag couldn't pour water out of a boot if the instructions were printed on the heel. "You must have him confused with someone else," I say through gritted teeth. I have a hard time imagining my father spending all our money in a saloon. I'm pretty sure he's a rich cowboy or exploring the wilds of the North Pole, unable to contact us because of life-or-death matters or because he's been sworn to secrecy by a Russian tsar, facts that will all be proven when I find him.

"May I help you, Margaret?" Mama asks in a very-not-helpful voice. She grabs the letters from Mrs. Cavanaugh and immediately tucks them under her arm. Mrs. Cavanaugh seems a little taken aback at Mama's rudeness. Come to think of it, I'm a little surprised, too. Mama always says to love thy neighbor, but she is definitely not acting the part today.

"Not that it's any of your business," she continues, flipping through our mail, "but Arthur was indeed raised in Omaha. Since then, however, you could say he is from a lot of places. The letter, by the way, is from my cousin Bertha," she says, her voice as cold as the frost I like to scrape off the windows with my fingernail.

I scrape some frost off the window with my fingernail. Smoke from Indian Town slithers lazily off to the west, and two-story company houses line the street like dominoes. Mama says it's strange a lumber town like ours doesn't have a tree in sight, but when Mr. Weston, the boss of the entire Chicago and Weston Lumber Company, says to cut down the trees because he's afraid of fires, no one is about to argue.

I scrape off more frost and watch the guy on the boardwalk in front of the house, the one leaning against the Perkinses' cow, Buttermilk, while lighting his coffin nail for a smoke, and remember that my father could be anywhere, even here. That man could be my father! He could be waiting for me, ready to take me to Mr. Weston's office to talk about man stuff, or to the general store to buy some bullets to shoot tin cans, or Mrs. Cavanaugh's pink underdrawers.

I watch the man's smoky breath. His hat is cockeyed, his wrinkly coat dirty and unbuttoned, one pant leg rolled halfway up, the other halfway down, a hand scratching his left butt cheek, a thread of brown spit landing on the road, melting into the dirty ice.

No, now that I think about it, that certainly could *not* be my father.

I have a feeling it's going to take a lot more than this to save that guy.

Mrs. Cavanaugh's voice jerks me to reality. "I see your mother has arrived, Alice. I'm sure you must be thrilled and delighted by Cora's unexpected visit." She looks at Mama eagerly.

"She's here to see us, Margaret. It's perfectly reasonable for a mother to visit her daughter and grandson, wouldn't you think?" Mama says icily, and turns to me. "Stan, thank Mrs. Cavanaugh and see her out, please."

"Thanks for this cracker jack pie, Mrs. Cavanaugh. It's our favorite. You really should give us the recipe," I say, ushering her toward the door.

Mrs. Cavanaugh stops short. "Well, Stan, I can surely see you all could use a little more meat on your bones, what with money being scarce. Just doing Christian charity for my fellow human beings in need. And by the way"—she leans in—"what in the world is up with that mother of yours?"

"I have no idea what you mean, ma'am." I open the front door and gently push Mrs. Cavanaugh through it. I know, however, exactly what she means. Ever since the arrival of that mysterious envelope, Mama has not exactly been acting like herself. Then again, I haven't quite been acting like myself, either.

CHAPTER 4

My breath appears like a ghost in front of me when I enter my room—the heat from the woodstove seems to have lost its way to this part of the house and the window leaks cold air, even through the rags Mama stuffed into the cracks. I sit on my bed, turn up the wick on my kerosene lamp, and take the Scrapbook from my bedside table, flipping through to find an empty spot.

My new tube of glue makes me as happy as picking a scab, but to be perfectly clear, I much prefer library paste.

Mama has forbidden its purchase, however, since I may have tasted the tiniest bit of it a long time ago when I was little. This new glue doesn't taste nearly as good.

Or so I've been told.

I place the envelope firmly next to a picture for the bang-up new bike I will be requesting for my birthday. When I saw the advertisement, I made sure to show it to Mama in case she didn't know what to get me. "Stan," she said, "you just had your birthday two weeks ago." Like that was important.

"It's always good to be prepared," I replied. Because that right there is the gospel truth. Plus, eleven months and seventeen days can go by very quickly. Except when it doesn't, like when you're waiting for your twelfth birthday.

When Granny saw the picture, she made a sound like air was leaking from her ears. "Pfft. I'm not sure about this fly-by-night contraption. Just seems like another thing Stan could kill himself on. It's not safe, Alice." Granny's voice was dark with warning.

I gave Mama a charming, sweet smile, the kind no one can ever resist. Except maybe Granny, and she doesn't count because she doesn't know a good thing when she sees it.

"Mama," I said, "you know I'm the safest almost-twelve-year-old in the Upper Peninsula of Michigan. Why, remember when I saved Lydia Mae from that wolf?" I blinked innocently.

"First of all, you're barely eleven," Mama responded. "And are you perhaps referring to the time you ran screaming from Mrs. Cavanaugh's doorstep when her toy poodle, Snookums, showed up at the door, and you grabbed Lydia's hand from fright and pulled her halfway around the block?"

"Well, she didn't get bitten, did she?" I grumped, and stomped off to my room.

The same room Granny enters right now without knocking. "Here's a satchel. Start packing. Your uncle Carl will be here at four-thirty."

"Today? Why?" I squeak. I'm feeling a bit bamboozled. The last time Uncle Carl set foot in this house was to deliver Granny like an unwanted package, so it's understandable if I'm not exactly looking forward to his appearance.

Unless he's coming to pick her up, in which case he is most welcome.

"Listen. You are eleven years old and somewhat the man of the house." Granny thinks for a minute when she says this, like she's not quite sure it's true, then takes a deep breath and continues anyway.

"You are old enough to know money has become increasingly tight and a situation has arisen"—she says the word "situation" like it is written in fancy letters—"making it both desirable and necessary for us to spend some time at your uncle Henry's logging camp."

"What?" I look at her like she has just grown fangs, which, to be perfectly honest, is a rather strong possibility.

Sure, Mama has been stingy with the kerosene for our

lamps and I've had to heat up baked beans for dinner more often than I'd like, but Granny is uttering a shovelful of poppycock. Also, that logging camp is awfully far away in Grand Marais. Lydia Mae said her uncle Charlie went there last year and never returned.

"That was last year's camp, Stan," Granny says. "The Grand Marais camp has no more trees to fell. Your uncle Henry's camp is closer to Germfask, about four hours from here." She gazes off through the frosty window. "Four . . . cold . . . hours from here," she mutters, half to herself.

A lumber camp. With real lumberjacks. I'll admit I paid little attention to Uncle Henry and Aunt Lois when they passed through in October. And I paid absolutely *no* attention to their devious daughter, Geri, who tried to frame me for everything from starting a fire in the dried leaves out back to breaking the window in the kitchen. I vaguely gathered they were headed to a lumber camp filled with masses of men carrying sharp axes and snaggletoothed saws, but the few times a year I am graced with Geri's presence, I must stay so alert, so on my toes, I can't focus on anything else. I do recall thinking those lumberjacks surely had no idea what was in store for them with Geri wandering around camp. Nine times out of ten, she is up to no good, and I will be surprised if that camp is still standing by the time we roll in.

"Thanks for the invitation, Granny, but I can't leave Manistique. I have some big plans and friends who will miss me, and I will be happy to quit school and get a job to help with any money problems," I say reasonably. I am not thinking about myself here. Conrad McAllister won't get a lick of exercise if I'm gone—who will he run after at the end of the school day? And it really is too much to ask Lydia Mae to eat all her lunch by herself. Someone needs to help her with the delicious stew her mom packs in her dinner pail, and don't get me started on the baking-powder biscuits. Without me, Lydia Mae would weigh at least three hundred pounds.

Granny looks at me. She is not amused. "Stan, I am not amused. You, believe it or not, have no say in the matter. Sometimes we have to do what is best for everyone involved, not just ourselves."

Sometimes it seems like I'm *always* forced to do what's best for everyone else involved. When will it be time to do what's best for me? And who exactly is going to this lumber camp? Granny and me? "Does this have something to do with that envelope I saw lying around?" I ask.

"Why?" Granny asks intently. "You've seen it, haven't

you? Where is it?" Her eyes lose focus. "If I could just see that postmark again, I'd remember exactly where in Texas that low-down, unreliable excuse for a man was last seen. . . ."

Would she track him down? Do I want Granny to track him down? I quietly close my Scrapbook lying on the bed behind me. Talk about unreliable—Granny already lost my father once; who's to say she won't lose him again? Plus, it's completely possible she would scare him away. "Woman, I have no idea what you are talking about. So, four-thirty, eh?"

Granny eyes me suspiciously. "In the morning. We need to arrive in time to make lunch," she says. "Pack everything, because it's so cold up there even the squirrels wear knickers." I gasp. I have never before heard that woman mention something so unladylike, and she continues as if the word "knickers" comes out of her mouth daily. "The three of us will be stuck in the camp cook shanty for the winter, so be prepared."

I am beginning to put two and two together, and it equals approximately three and one half. This little chat has cleared up some of the conversation I overheard. I now understand the talk about a "fresh start" and "money" and "camp," but I'm still not sure about my father's connection to all this, and I am utterly befuddled about the pickle. There is a 56.9 percent possibility that

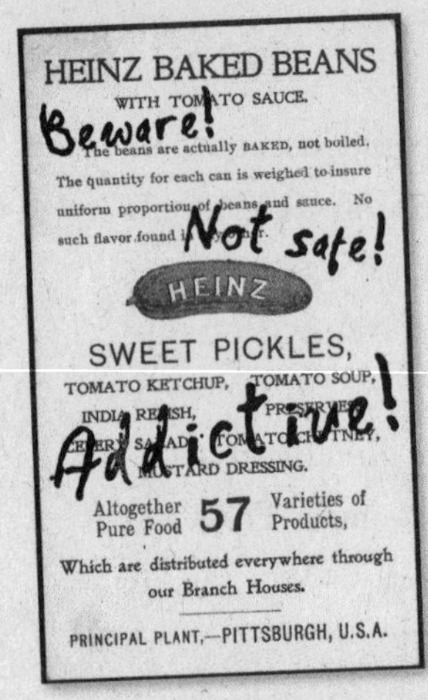

Granny is planning on selling me and using the money to support a bad pickle habit. But I'm 43.1 percent not sure about that.

At least I know I won't be alone with Granny. That right there is worthy of a sigh of relief. But with the prospect of Granny in my life for the next few months, it now seems very possible I might not live to see the spring. She might be little, but she's one tough cookie who loves to remind everyone that "if you spare the rod, you spoil the child." Usually she says this while slapping a wooden spoon on her palm and staring in my direction.

I make a list of some of the times Granny has disciplined me on the off chance I can avoid these situations a second time:

1. I made the keen observation that Lydia Mae was a mewling, beetle-headed malt worm. Between you and me, she's not. I like her dark curls, and I actually wouldn't know a malt worm if it bit me on the kazoo.

2. I licked the butter. In my defense, don't leave the butter on the counter if you don't want someone to lick it.

3. I yelled, "Gee whiz!" Honestly, it was not my fault that Reverend Sherman scared the bejeebers out of

me. Lydia Mae had told me a terrifying loup-garou story the day before, and I might have been a little bit tired from lack of sleep. I was walking down Main Street, minding my own business, kicking a rock, when the good Reverend jumped from behind a pole. He has a big beard that looks a little wolfish, if you squint and the light is just right. He told Granny I had "taken the Lord's name in vain," but I think grown men shouldn't jump at kids from behind poles. And they should have a sense of humor. And trim their beards.

All those things happened just yesterday.

I grab my other pair of trousers, my two flannel shirts, and my woolen union suit and stuff them in the satchel along with another pair of socks. I remind myself not to forget my toy soldiers as I pick up my Scrapbook to stick it in the bag.

I can't help opening the Scrapbook again, carefully keeping one eye on the door. The mysterious envelope has a stamp, my mama's name, "Manistique, MI" scrawled in a slant across the bottom, and that Texas postmark. Would it be possible to get to Texas and find him? Would he still be there? Or would I end up in Texas looking for my father while he is in Michigan looking for me?

I realize my father held this very same envelope in his hands, hands that might look a lot like mine. I slide my finger across the opening and peer inside. For something so empty, it holds so many questions.

Who is my father? Where is my father? Why did he leave us? Could it be he doesn't want a son?

Nah. That can't be it.

Maybe, aside from being lost, he has been really busy with important, top-secret business. Or trapped. Or on tour with a famous traveling show, one that only stops at towns with really bad post offices. I can just imagine the letters he would have written, all of them probably lost in the mail:

Dear Stan,

I'm sorry you have not received the hundreds of letters I've sent since you were born. I was in Mexico fighting bulls with Vincente Oropeza but found I just don't have the heart for killing an animal, and folks quickly get tired of watching a fellow in fancy breeches being chased by a bull.

So when Vincente left to join Buffalo Bill Cody's Wild West show, I decided to go with him. It turns out I am a natural with the lasso and can hit a target with an arrow even blindfolded with both hands tied behind my back.

I'm quite famous, but being famous doesn't mean the post office will deliver your letters, apparently.

I will be sending you a blindfold, a bull, and tickets to the next show we have in Michigan.

From,
Dad
aka Big Shot Buckaroo

That's got to be what happened. It makes perfect sense.

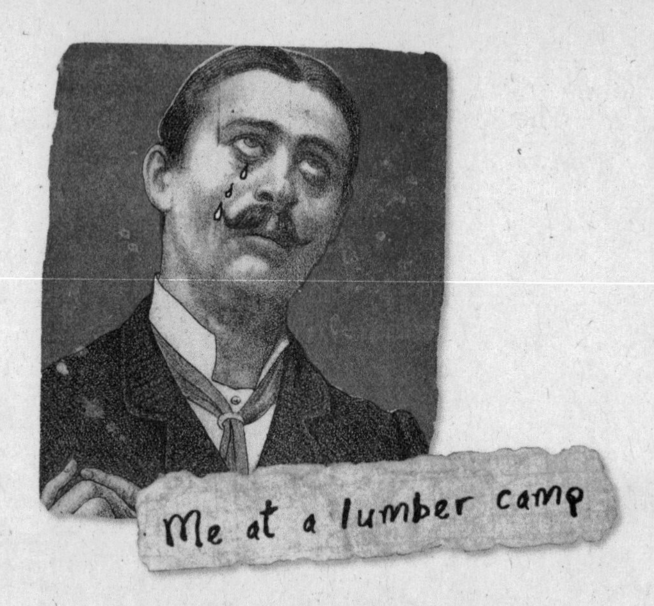

CHAPTER 5

Mama's voice cuts through the darkness, sharp and crisp. "I'm rethinking this entire plan, Mother," I hear her say. "There's no logical reason for me to drag Stan away from school to a rough-and-tumble logging camp in the middle of nowhere. If nothing else, he'll be bored to tears and underfoot."

"My dear," Granny says in a voice that certainly does *not* feel "dear," "we've already gone over all of this. May I remind you that you have the tendency to fret over the wrong things? You can't sustain your current work hours and keep a watchful eye on that boy of yours; he's spending much too much time unsupervised. Who knows what kind of trouble he's been getting into? Just last week I saw him throwing snowballs at that nice McAllister boy. Plus, I think it's more important to concentrate on how you're planning to feed yourself and Stan."

Even through the layers of blankets I can feel the rumble of my empty stomach. Someone does need to feed me, that goes without saying. And someone needed to throw snowballs at that "nice McAllister boy," too. He had it coming to him after he asked me if my name was Maple Syrup and then called me a sap.

"Without the additional money from Arthur coming in," Granny continues, "you can't keep food on the table and a roof over your heads. This job at the lumber camp will pay three times as much as you make at the general store, and you'll have the support of family besides. And I am more than happy to sacrifice my time until you have a man to look after you and keep Stan in line."

We don't need some random man to take care of us! Mama and I have done just fine on our own, thank you very much. And what about Granny complimenting my "somewhat" manliness just yesterday—has she forgotten this so soon? And isn't she the one who let me believe my father was dead and then offered no help finding him? She is well aware I already have a father. I poke my head out of the covers to shout a reminder but catch my breath in the cold.

I'll remind her later. And remind myself to act even manlier than I normally do.

"Stan will not be bored," she says. "In fact, I practically

guarantee it." I hear a threat in her words, but I can't hear Mama's mumbled reply because of the banging and scraping that interrupts Granny's huffy lecture.

Apparently Mama's reply wasn't enough, because six hours and fourteen minutes later, I'm shivering under a worn, woolen blanket, my knees knocking together with each bump of the sleigh over the icy dirt road. Mama sits up front with Uncle Carl, both shadows against the teeth-chattering dark, leaving me with Granny in the back.

Crates holding our belongings crush my feet. I try to make room to stretch my legs when my hand brushes against something furry. I'm pretty sure it's a cat. Or Granny's leg. Her hairy loup-garou leg.

I glance at the too-early morning moon, sifting through clouds as we slip our way out of town. It's only a fingernail, so we're safe. For now.

"Safe from what?" Granny demands. Her voice is as unpleasant as a spoonful of cod-liver oil. "You're not still in a stew over that loup-garou story, are you? Because I am not having you waking me up at all hours with nightmares again, you hear me?"

A couple days ago, Lydia Mae told me how her uncle Charlie was a loup-garou and ate everything he came across during a full moon. He tried to gobble up Lydia Mae's aunt Martha, but she hit him over the head with a broom and immediately left to go live with her sister in Duluth. I asked Lydia Mae why I hadn't heard about that little happening, and she claimed it took place in San Francisco or somewhere.

Basically, I think she's a liar, but after I spotted a stray hair on Granny's chin, I'll admit I haven't been able to sleep very well.

Now that I'm the newly appointed "somewhat" man of the house, however, that behavior is over. "Pshaw, old lady," I mutter. "I never did that. You must have been dreaming."

"Don't be so rude. And anyway, that's complete balderdash. The Lord does not bless a lie, Stanley," she scolds. "Now, while you're poking around for who-knows-what, find my muff. My hands are cold."

I'm dutifully pushing some boxes around when I pinch

my fingers in the hinge of a crate. "Drat!" I cry. Before I can say Jack Robinson, Granny reaches out and grabs my ear.

"Dad-blame it, woman! That hurts!" I wail. It's true. Granny's fingers are like a crab's claws. "I can see stars!"

"That's for your horrible language, young man. Don't let me hear such profanity again," Granny warns as I rub my ear. "And of course you can see stars. You're in the dark, surrounded by them."

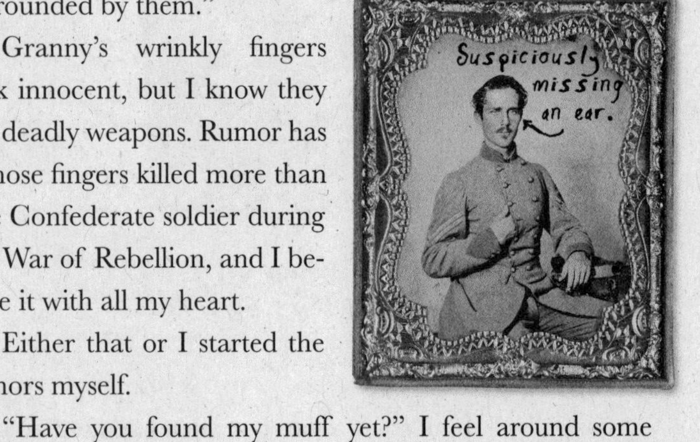

Granny's wrinkly fingers look innocent, but I know they are deadly weapons. Rumor has it those fingers killed more than one Confederate soldier during the War of Rebellion, and I believe it with all my heart.

Either that or I started the rumors myself.

"Have you found my muff yet?" I feel around some more and finally come upon a ball of fur. I give it to Granny and she tucks her hands into each end.

"Now, for the love of Pete, can you please just shut that trap of yours so we can rest a bit before we get to camp?" It sounds like a question, but we both know it's an order.

She's pure evil.

Mama says no one is 100 percent evil, but I'm not so sure about that. If I think about it, I can remember one time when Granny spit on her hankie to wipe jelly off my face, which is kind of disgusting but also kind of nice, depending on how you look at it. And if you ignore the spitting part. So maybe Granny is only 99.9 percent evil.

Uncle Carl hums through the cold. He says humming takes his mind off his troubles. I can't imagine what troubles he has, however. He lives down the street from us, alone, as in no bossy women around, and works for the lumber company, carting supplies and people to and from the camps. What could be easier? Plus, when Granny comes to visit, she stays with us, and Uncle Carl can escape her anytime he wants.

Icicles cling to his beard and his breath forms little clouds that rise up in the thin moonlight. He has said three things since we got on this sleigh: "Hey!" "Oof!" and "Yah!" When I get to that logging camp and pick up my ax, I'm going to be like Uncle Carl, except with a lot more words. I will start a life of adventure, like my dad, and will be a lone wolf, taking care of myself and Mama. And I might grow a beard, chew tobacco, and drink coffee. And understand things apparently only men can understand. The first step of my plan is to . . .

"Okay, okay." Granny sits up quickly and straightens her bonnet. "Stop blathering on and on and tell me your plan already. Then can we get some sleep?"

"What makes you think I'm planning anything?" I ask. I've got to stop blurting things out.

"I'll tell you what you should plan on doing: practicing

discipline, learning your lessons, and honing your manners, as well as forgetting any foolish notions involving that father of yours. These next few months will be a great opportunity to work on being less dramatic, impertinent, and impolite. Not to mention less ridiculous."

Surprisingly, this is not what I have in mind, unless by "less dramatic, impertinent, and impolite," she means "more adventurous, manly, and dangerous." I have no idea what she means by "ridiculous."

"I know this is not what you have in mind," Granny continues, "and that's exactly why we will be working on improving the evil aspects of your nature."

Who is *she* calling evil? Just because I have a taste for danger doesn't mean I'm evil. Believe you me, I know evil by name, probably because it's sitting right across from me. And its name rhymes with "Fanny."

"We will also work on your inability to hold your tongue and use proper English. I cannot abide the slang you toss out of that mouth of yours like spit on a frying pan."

I think about spitting on a frying pan.

Granny keeps talking about all my shameful habits. I'm disrespectful. I eat too much and too loudly. My hair is unruly. I don't bathe often enough. Blah, blah, blah.

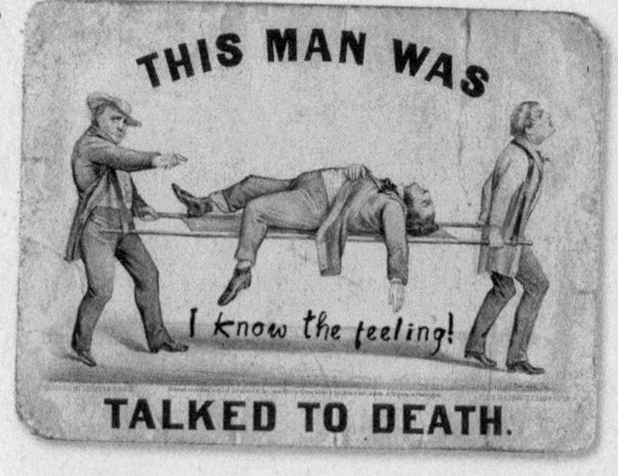

"Please and thank you can get you a long way, and proper table manners should never be taken for granted. You'd be surprised how something as simple as using the correct spoon can open doors that might otherwise remain shut."

I imagine jimmying open a stuck door using a spoon. I am pretty sure the spoon would bend, and maybe even break, but I will not be sharing this thought with Granny. If she wants to go around breaking spoons in doors, that's her business.

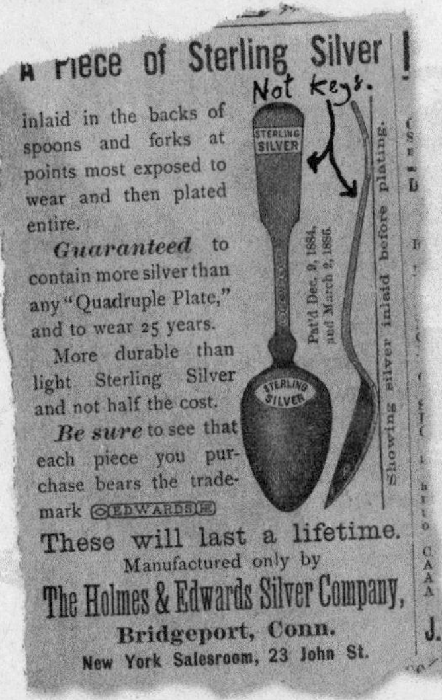

Her words grate like a sliver under a fingernail, and I don't know how much longer I can suffer the woman's torture. I have never before had the urge to commit an act of lawlessness, but Granny's voice might force me to give up my law-abiding ways, skip town, and start a life of crime.

STAN MAN

~~BILLY~~ THE ~~KID~~

$500 Reward

DEAD OR ALIVE

"And how might you plan on skipping town?" Granny asks.

"Why?" I respond.

"Well, I'm not planning on stopping you, if that's what you're worried about." She seems awfully lackadaisical about the fact that her only grandson may soon be running away to join a band of outlaws.

"First of all, they would never take you." Granny's body rocks with the wagon like a puppet on a string.

I snort. "What are you talking about? Have you seen me handle a gun? I am a whiz at the gun handling, I don't mind saying."

"You've never handled a gun, Stanley," Granny says.

I begin to protest, but then remember it's true. The only gun I ever handled was a cap gun, and even then I had to borrow it from Lydia Mae.

"And you get scared when we walk down Maple Street and your mother isn't holding your hand."

That only happened once.

"Last week," Granny reminds me. To be fair, Mama had slipped on the icy road and I was just lending a hand to help her balance. "And

we're deep in the woods. It would take you days walking to get anywhere near civilization. You'd be wolf food before you got that far, I suspect."

I shudder. I'm not sure what to expect for the next few months, but hopefully it does not include my becoming wolf food.

I prefer to be the one doing the eating, thank you very much.

We weave through the woods, tunneling among the trees. The farther away from town we get, the less of a road we seem to be following and the more the forest seems to swallow us, only occasionally letting in a thread of moonlight. Apparently we're just trusting the horses to get us where we need to go.

Branches rasp the side of the sleigh, grabby tentacles reaching in. Every once in a while we pass large, scarred areas of stumps scattered like gravestones. More trees. An abandoned logging camp falling in on itself in the shadows. Roads that still bear ax wounds.

Something scrapes up my back like bony fingers, my collar tightens, and I feel myself being lifted from the sleigh. If wolves don't get me, apparently skeletons will. Granny's head snaps in my direction so sharply her bones click in place. Whatever is trying to grab me should go for her instead, because I am sure as eggs are eggs, anything that tries to attack Granny will have the worse end of that deal.

Plus, I'm almost positive she has rabies.

Granny reaches toward me, her bony fingers coming closer, most likely ready to pluck an eyeball out of my head. I scrunch my eyes up real tight. None of my options right about now seem very good, so I am going to have to hope for the least painful death.

And that's when Granny pulls a branch from behind my neck.

"My, aren't we overdramatic," she says. Her voice is flat, as if nothing scary has just happened. As if I didn't almost lose my life.

Uncle Carl turns around. "Branch getcha?" It sounds like the hint of a smile might be lurking at the edge of his mouth.

I straighten up. "I got everything handled here, Uncle Carl. Don't you worry." And I wink at him, man-to-man style. He can't see me since my eye is covered with my hat and it's still very dark, but we men have our own secret language. He knows.

"You okay?" Mama turns her head, her eyes searching my face.

"Pfft," I reply. The little lady shouldn't worry herself over any of it.

Me and my new underdrawers!

"Alice, you have got to get that boy's imagination under control," I hear Granny huff to Mama, but my mind drifts to the horses' hooves and their snorting breath. I'm not even sure that's exactly what she says. I'm feeling a little foggy. Maybe she says, "You have got to get that boy new underdrawers and send him to the North Pole."

Or even, "You have got to wipe the snot off that boy's nose."

I glance at Mama. She's haloed in horse breath and her head nods to the beat of their hooves. Uncle Carl hums, but I don't think his humming is enough to put a smile back on Mama's face.

Uncle Carl really can't carry a tune.

CHAPTER 6

I was not sleeping. And I most certainly was not drooling. Babies drool. Lydia Mae's little brother Charlie, he's a baby and he's disgusting. And he drools.

Plus, once I caught him eating my shoe.

It was still on my foot.

I sneak a peek at Granny. Her little beady birdie eyes stare at me.

"Is that drool?" she asks.

"Sheesh!" I look away and casually wipe my face with my itchy mitten, the one Granny knitted. I don't know where someone would find yarn as scratchy as sandpaper, but Granny apparently did. "You are seeing things. You need to get yourself some eyeglasses." I cautiously raise my head and sit up.

"I am wearing eyeglasses."

I squint my eyes to examine her face more closely. "Oh. Well . . ." How did I miss something so obvious as glasses? "Then it's clear you need new ones."

"Look, Stan." Uncle Carl points. "Camp." He throws words over his shoulder like he has to pay money to use them.

Pencils of smoke rise up from shacks at the edge of the forest. The dawn is pewter, and the surrounding woods are a smudgy outline.

I don't know what I expected, but it wasn't this. The lumber camp makes Manistique look like New York City. Or what I imagine New York City looks like from the postcard Mama's other brother, Uncle Erick, sent last year: every inch of the photo is filled with life—sidewalks of people, streets with horses and carriages, tall buildings with waving flags, moving and swaying, folks buzzing along like bees around a hive.

Uncle Erick went to the big city to make his fortune, but when I told that to Granny, she mumbled, "More like drink away his fortune."

I don't know how you drink a fortune, but it had better taste really good.

What I see before me now is a hodgepodge of tar-paper shacks, apparently slapped together with whatever was lying about, plunked down willy-nilly around a snow-covered clearing. The camp is quiet but for the clop of our horses and the ping of metal on metal coming from a building off in the distance. Everything appears abandoned but for the capped chimneys poking out from roofs, smoke popping the caps and then freezing in the cold air.

It all reminds me of Mr. Weston, the banker. I sit behind him and his bald head in church. And right now I feel like

I'm in the middle of Mr. Weston's bald spot surrounded by a scraggly fringe of forest.

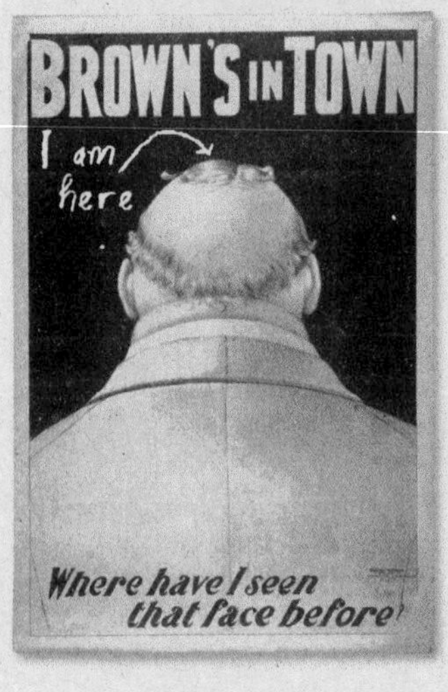

The camp is horribly quiet. Where are the cows running loose through the streets or the chickens tripping you up as you stumble off to school? At home, all sorts of sounds greet you in the morning and sing you to sleep. The creaky tram car sends chills up your spine, while down by the water, scows chug out in the bay to dump sawdust into Lake Michigan. And through it all is the hum of the sawmill. Granny says silence is golden, but for me, when things are quiet, it just means someone needs to make some noise.

Mama turns, gathers the blankets covering our laps, and starts folding them.

"So when we pull into camp, should I start sharpening axes? Chopping some wood? Cutting down trees?" I ask eagerly. Forest surrounds the camp, so I know my help is definitely needed. These lumberjacks don't even have the sense to chop down the trees right in front of them.

"No!" Mama and Granny immediately answer together. It's the first time I've ever thought they really are related. "For one thing, these trees aren't worth the effort to cut them down." Granny waves at the woods surrounding us. "They're all hardwoods."

"Anyway, Geri will want to show you around the camp," Mama says softly as she straightens my hat. The mention of my cousin makes me about as nervous as a june bug in a henhouse. When I last saw her in October, I ended up limping for a week and had nightmares for a month.

Granny spins me to face her and ties my scarf like she is tightening a noose. "No axes for you," she pronounces.

Clearly very safe.

"Would you consider a little saw?" I attempt to negotiate.

"No." Granny turns to Mama, dismissing me. "We'll drop off our bags, the boys will unload the wagon, and we'll head to the kitchen and help your sister get the lunches ready. Carl?" My uncle leans his head back to indicate he's listening. "How far off are the shanty boys working this week?"

"Well, when I was here on delivery last week, they were a couple miles west. Take about an hour to get the lunch sleigh to 'em."

Granny arches her eyebrows. "So plan on that, Alice."

Mama says nothing. Or maybe, like me, she's just too tired to argue.

My stomach growls. "Is it time to eat?" I ask hopefully.

Granny scoffs, "No. It's long past breakfast."

How can that possibly be true? The sun is barely making

an appearance, my eyes still sting from napping, and if I don't get food soon I will surely waste away to nothing.

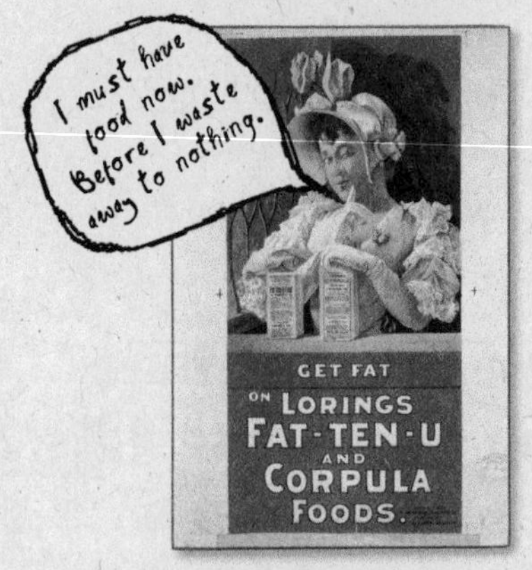

"The boys have been in the woods for hours already. You'll have to scavenge for something in the cook shanty, but don't get underfoot." She shakes a finger at me.

Above the steady beat of the horses' hooves, coyotes howl in the distance. At least I hope they're coyotes. I think of the lumberjacks—the shanty boys—out in the woods for hours already. I'm not so sure cutting down trees in the dark is such a good idea. What if you think you're cutting down a tree but you accidentally cut off someone's head? I'm almost positive that happens.

Innocent victim of an "actual" beheading.

Granny looks at me blankly. "When would you suggest they cut them down? It's dark for fourteen hours a day this time of year. You want the shanty boys to fell trees in the summer when the days are longer? How do you think they would get the logs to the river? Carry them on their backs? Pull them through the muddy swamps? No, Stan, they need the icy roads. It's the ice that enables the horses to pull the loaded sleighs to the river. By the way, lest we forget, it's also the stuff you insist upon sticking your tongue to at least twice a week."

Everyone loves a sarcastic grandmother.

She also exaggerates. I only got my tongue stuck once last week. And it surely wasn't on an icy road. It was on the metal horse-head hitching post outside the general store, which anyone in his right mind would agree is hard to resist.

"Um, Ma, you do know some of the camps run through the summer, right?" Uncle Carl quietly suggests.

Granny is not terribly fond of being corrected. "And how exactly do they manage that?" she scoffs.

"Those big wheel thingamabobs like what they got at camps down near Saginaw. They make it so you can pull the loads through the swamps and not sink in."

"Well," Granny responds, "do we have them at this camp?"

"No. Too expensive," Uncle Carl responds. "And Henry only runs this camp through the spring."

"Then they might as well not exist," Granny says, and we all know that's the end of that.

I realize with a shudder that it's getting close to the end of me, too, because running toward us like a black wave of death is something even more frightening than a loup-garou during a full moon.

Geri.

1,000 CHOICE LIVE TURKEYS WANTED.

A Grand Line of Useful and Sensible Christmas Presents at Low Prices.

With each purchase of $7 50 or more we give a Fine Christmas Turkey free, which also entitles the buyer to three guesses for our Three Valuable Gifts, as each purchase of $2 50 entitles you to a guess. The patron guessing the nearest number of buttons in glass jar receives the Pony, the second nearest the Bicycle and the third nearest the Gold Watch.

LAST CALL.

Do not lose sight of the fact that we bought every Seal and Persian Lamb Cap that Gillespie, Ansley & Martin, 58 and 60 Wellington St. W., had in their warehouse. We are selling them at prices so low, buy you surely will. Genuine South Sea Seal Caps, worth $18, at $10. Genuine Persian Lamb Caps, worth $7, at $2 50. Imitation Persian Lambs (all sizes), worth $2, at 50c. Imitation Persian Lamb Caps, worth $1 50, at 25c.

GENTS' FURNISHINGS.

Neckwear, Hosiery, Silk Handkerchiefs, Collars, Cuffs, Underwear, Braces, Umbrellas, Cuff Buttons, Collar Buttons, Scarf Pins, Links, etc., etc. All the Newest and most Nobby Styles. No other establishment in Canada can duplicate the array of Serviceable and Sensible Presents at the prices we quote. Make your selection early and secure the Newest and Choicest Goods.

P. JAMIESON,

The Leading Men's, Youths', Boys' and Children's Outfitter in Canada.

CHAPTER 7

Geri jumps up on the side of the wagon as we clop slowly into camp. Her coppery braids are a mess, and her apron, half buttoned into her wool coat, flutters up and down in the cold air. Mama thinks she's as pure as the driven snow and as innocent as a newly laid egg. She's older than me by only twenty-three months and three days, but she acts as if she learned all the world's secrets during that short time. And apparently I have to go through her to find them out.

"Geraldine." Granny nods.

"Hey, Granny." Geri smiles. She flings her arms over the side of the wagon, her feet dangling off the ground.

"Hello, Grandmother," Granny corrects.

Mama pats Geri's unruly hair, holding herself steady with her other hand while the horses come to a stop. Geri looks at me with her head tilted to the side.

"Are you feeling okay?" she asks, her voice full of concern. It's the first time we've seen each other in three months and that's all she can say?

"Huh? Yeah. Why?"

"Um, no reason. You just look a little yellow. No headache? Do you feel like you need to throw up? Do your muscles ache? Are you feverish?"

"No! Why?" It's against my better judgment to listen to a word Geri says, but the last time I didn't heed her warning, my tongue got stuck to the flagpole outside the Ossawinamakee Hotel. I've been trying to prove her wrong ever since, which is why my tongue has been stuck to almost every metal thing in Schoolcraft County. Also, I'm starting to feel a little queasy the more she talks, and maybe a bit warm. I take off my mitten just in case, and am pretty sure my hand is slightly yellow.

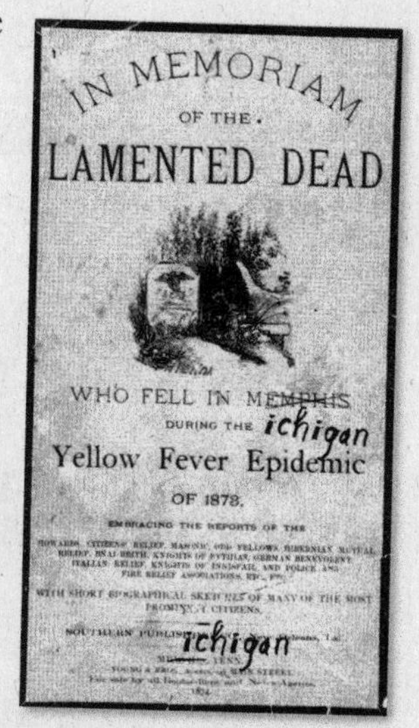

"Geraldine," Granny says sternly, "that's enough. Stan does not have yellow fever."

Yellow fever? Did Granny say I have yellow fever? I might be seconds away from death's door, miles and miles from any type of doctor, and my dead body will probably have to be stored in a shed until the frozen ground softens enough to bury my poor, decaying remains. This is not the way I envisioned my death! How will my sweet mama carry on without the "somewhat" man of the house around?

Granny looks at me over her eyeglasses and sighs. "I said, you do *not* have yellow fever. Which means you are *not* dying. Now, if you don't mind the inconvenience, let's get on with living. Help your uncle Carl unload."

Geri shrugs, grins at me, and plops off the side of the wagon.

I am unexpectedly grateful to Granny for saving my life from yellow fever, even if it turned out *not* to be yellow fever, so I decide to lower her Evil Rating to 99.4 percent.

"Stan, toss me your turkey." Geri holds her arms up as if waiting for something.

I'm so sick of women ordering me around, and what in the blazes is she talking about? What kind of ridiculous person travels for hours in a wagon filled with all his earthly possessions, minus the toy soldiers he forgot on the windowsill, while holding on to a turkey?

"I was talking about your satchel, you chowderhead. Up here they're called turkeys. If you're spending the winter at camp, you need to know these things. But if you want to carry it yourself, fine by me." Geri reaches out to help Mama step down from the wagon.

"Um, I knew that. I was just, uh, joshing you." Plus, I didn't mean to say it out loud.

"Sure you were," Geri says smugly. As I look around, I have the sad realization that with no one else my age around this camp, I'm going to have to find a way to get along with her. Or avoid her. And at some point she will need to learn this is a man's world, and I'm a man. And she's not.

"I'm not what?" Geri looks at me expectantly.

"A man," I reply. I hate to be so frank, but she's going to have to learn her place sometime.

"Thank the good Lord for that!" Geri exclaims.

Huh? Does she have to be so confusing?

"They always are," Uncle Carl whispers. He motions for me to help unload the wagon, and I start passing him crates and boxes.

"Oof! What's in this one again?" Uncle Carl gasps, dropping the box to the ground.

"Granny's magazines, books, and old newspapers, remember?"

"Oh, yep. That's a woman who needs her reading materials, eh?"

Ain't that the truth. *Harper's Weekly, The Atlantic Monthly, St. Nicholas,* newspapers and anything else with printed letters. The best part of having a Granny who hoards reading materials, besides how they keep her busy for hours on end, is when she's done she lets me cut out advertisements and articles and pictures and paste them in my Scrapbook. Sometimes she lets me cut things out *before* she's done reading, but I don't think she's caught on to that little trick yet.

I think I'll change her Evil Rating to 97.1 percent while I have the chance.

Granny makes her way over to what I guess will be our sleeping quarters. She carries nothing but her head held high and her ratty old purse. She looks like she should be walking down the steps of a castle rather than the dirty, icy street of a lumber camp.

"Does she think she's the Queen of England?" Geri asks, nodding in Granny's direction.

I shrug.

"Let's throw these trunks and crates into your room, and then I'll show you around." Geri grabs me and pulls me closer. "If we can't be found," she whispers, "we won't have to help with supper."

My stomach growls. "I'm hungry," I say.

"Oh, stop whining." Geri reaches into her apron and takes out some bacon. "Here, eat this." Even though she called me a whiner and I really should thump her on the nose, I take a few slices. Honestly, I don't know when I'll get another chance to eat. Plus, it's bacon, and who can say no to bacon? In the back of my mind, however, I can't help wondering what kind of person keeps bacon in her pocket.

Geri tears off a piece with her teeth and sticks the rest in

The Author in Fancy Dress as a Side of Bacon, designed by himself, which took the First Prize of Forty Guineas at the Covent Garden Fancy Dress Ball, April 1894.

her apron. "C'mon." We grab each end of a trunk and follow Mama and Uncle Carl toward a group of cabins. Geri hauls me around back.

"We do not want to go in the front," she hisses. "It's the cook shanty. Your beds are in here." She nods at a door. "And don't make eye contact. If you do, they'll automatically ask you to do something like chop the firewood. Or pick up horse manure." She shudders at the thought.

We drag the crate inside just in time to see Mama and Uncle Carl come through a different door, probably the door to the kitchen, the one I want to avoid.

"Stan, we'll put you on the top bunk, and Granny and I

will share the bottom one," Mama says wearily. She looks as tired as I feel, her eyes flat and rimmed in red, but she simply sighs a little, drops her things to the floor, and heads to the kitchen. Uncle Carl tips his cap and makes for the door.

"Where are you going, Uncle Carl?" I ask, a little afraid to be left alone with Geri. Last time that didn't end up so great. Right before she set the leaves on fire, she dared me to light a match, even though Mama had strictly forbidden it.

I burned off part of my left eyebrow and a patch of hair that didn't grow in for a full two months. Conrad McAllister called me Baldilocks and kept asking me where my three bears were. Mama thanked the Lord nothing serious had happened, but then she didn't let me leave her sight for thirty-two and a half days.

And Geri got off scot-free.

Of course.

Uncle Carl slaps his cap on his scruffy head. "Just spending the night in the barn, then work has me in town till the river drive." He winks at us. "Wouldn't want to miss that, now would I?" Then he leaves.

I'm all at sea. "What is he talking about? What's the river drive?"

Geri looks at me like I've fallen out of the stupid tree and hit every branch on the way down.

"It's the most exciting event of the year, is all. It's better than if the circus and the county fair took place on Christmas Day." She leans in. "Only the best men, the river pigs, can drive the logs down the river. People line the banks to watch us parade by like they're cheering on the president himself. The main river fills with so many logs you can't see the water, and the men run over them like they're dancing across hot coals. One slip, however"—here she pauses dramatically—"and that river pig is food for the fishes, juggling halos, taking a dirt nap."

"Huh?" I ask, puzzled.

"He's dead, Stan," Geri says. Her voice clips the word "dead" like she killed him herself. "In the grave. Six feet under. Checked out."

It's a little worrisome how much Geri is enjoying this talk.

Hmmm. The river drive is so dangerous, men lose their lives. They could die. Dying makes me think about my dad, of course. It's still a little hard to believe he's not dead.

"Dead" also makes me think about coffins. Hey, what if my dad hasn't been able to write because he's been stuck in a coffin?

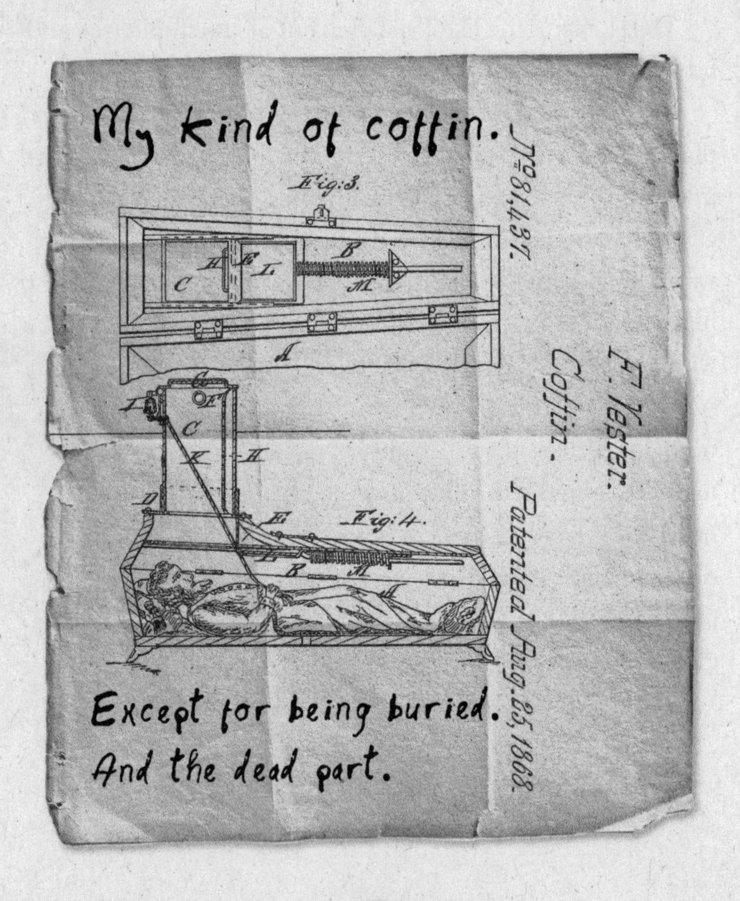

Dear Son,

I'm sorry I haven't written, but it's hard to write from inside a coffin. It's dark and stuffy and I didn't have a pen. If you ever find yourself in the position where you're about to be buried, remember a pen. And some paper. And a stamp. And a light of some sort probably wouldn't hurt.

It was very peaceful, however. In fact, not one woman told me what to do while I was in that thing. I will be sure to send you your very own burial case; it might be the only place you can find some peace and quiet.

From,
Dad

Geri leans on her heels looking smug. She thinks I'm scared. She thinks I'm afraid of death.

Truth is, I'm a little bit afraid of death. People die from it.

"And you should be," Geri says pointedly.

But not enough to stop me from going on the river drive. Nope. This is just the kind of adventure I've been looking for.

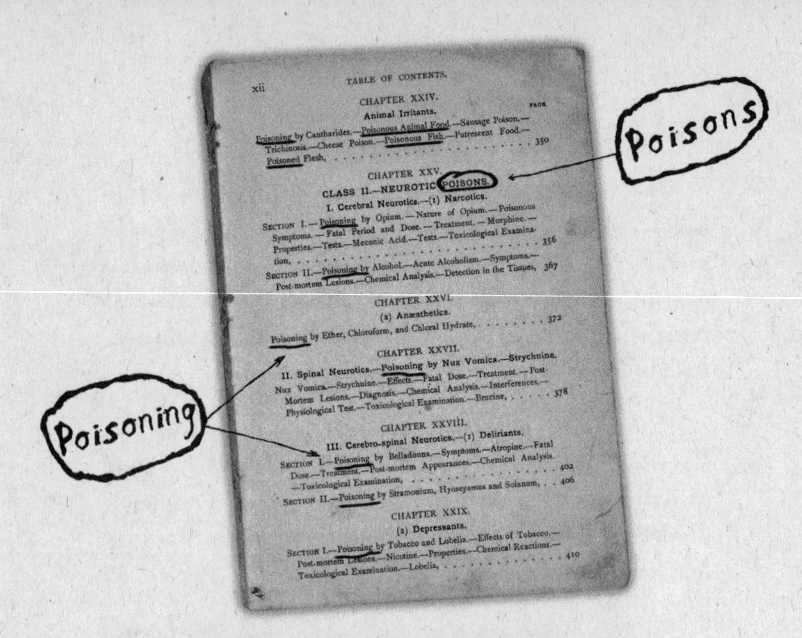

xii TABLE OF CONTENTS.

CHAPTER XXIV.

Animal Irritants.

PAGE

Poisoning by Cantharides.—Poisonous Animal Food.—Sausage Poison.—Trichinosis.—Cheese Poison.—Poisonous Fish.—Putrescent Food.—Poisoned Flesh, ... 350

CHAPTER XXV.

CLASS II.—NEUROTIC POISONS.

I. Cerebral Neurotics.—(1) Narcotics.

SECTION I.—Poisoning by Opium.—Nature of Opium.—Poisonous Symptoms.—Fatal Period and Dose.—Treatment.—Morphine.—Properties.—Tests.—Meconic Acid.—Tests.—Toxicological Examination, ... 356

SECTION II.—Poisoning by Alcohol.—Acute Alcoholism.—Symptoms.—Post-mortem Lesions.—Chemical Analysis.—Detection in the Tissues, 367

CHAPTER XXVI.

(2) Anæsthetics.

Poisoning by Ether, Chloroform, and Chloral Hydrate, ... 372

CHAPTER XXVII.

II. Spinal Neurotics.—Poisoning by Nux Vomica.—Strychnine.

Nux Vomica.—Strychnine.—Effects.—Fatal Dose.—Treatment.—Post-Mortem Lesions.—Diagnosis.—Chemical Analysis.—Interferences.—Physiological Test.—Toxicological Examination.—Brucine, ... 378

CHAPTER XXVIII.

III. Cerebro-spinal Neurotics.—(1) Deliriants.

SECTION I.—Poisoning by Belladonna.—Symptoms.—Atropine.—Fatal Dose.—Treatment.—Post-mortem Appearances.—Chemical Analysis.—Toxicological Examination, ... 402

SECTION II.—Poisoning by Stramonium, Hyoscyamus and Solanum, . . 406

CHAPTER XXIX.

(2) Depressants.

SECTION I.—Poisoning by Tobacco and Lobelia.—Effects of Tobacco.—Post-mortem Lesions.—Nicotine.—Properties.—Chemical Reactions.—Toxicological Examination.—Lobelia, ... 410

CHAPTER 8

So when does the river drive happen?" I ask, probably a little too eagerly.

"Oh, not for months. We have to wait until the ice roads start to melt and the river swells with the thaw. We've got lots of time." Geri waves a hand at me to swat the idea from my head. "Now let's drop your stuff and skedaddle." She grabs my turkey and tosses it up on my bunk. The straw from the mattress crunches under its weight.

"Where do you sleep?" I ask.

Geri puffs herself up a little, although she needs to straighten that hair of hers and button her coat correctly if she wants to start putting on airs.

"Well, you know Daddy is the foreman, which means he's basically the boss here. . . ." She pauses for effect. "So we, of course, have our own cabin behind the van." I must look puzzled. "You know, the office. I have my own bed. And a table for my medical books."

"Why in the Sam Hill," I can't help exclaiming, "would you, a girl, need medical books?"

Geri stares snootily at me, her hand on her hip. "Excuse me?"

I am dumbfounded. "Did you not know you're a girl?"

"Ahem."

It's Granny. Sakes alive, I hope she didn't hear me say "Sam Hill" or I'll be in a heap of trouble. No telling what she'll pinch this time.

"Oh, hey, Granny!" Geri exclaims through a mouthful of bacon.

"Hello, Grandmother," she corrects sternly. She pinches her lips together. "And your lack of manners will never get you a husband," she adds. Her words sound final, like a promise.

Geri chews more slowly and stares at Granny. She does not have a response.

As the one usually in trouble, I can't help grinning and thank the good Lord above that I've been spared. Also, anyone who can get Geri to shut her kisser earns a reduction in her Evil Rating. It is now a solid 96.3 percent.

Geri grabs my hand, smiles sweetly at Granny, and yanks me from the cabin.

There's nothing like Granny to instantly make your enemy your friend.

Geri drags me toward the center of camp, then grabs my shoulders and twirls me so I'm facing her directly. I have to look up a bit to meet her eyes, and she makes sure I do. "Listen, mister," she begins. I think she's waving a finger in my face, but with a mitten on, it's hard to tell. "I will ignore your ignorant remarks about my plans to become a doctor."

Mrs. M. L. Jordan, FEMALE?

MRS. M. L. JORDAN,
FEMALE PHYSICIAN,
No. 17 Portland Street,
(Corner of Garraux Place,) . . . BOSTON.
Hours for consultation and examination from 9 A.M. till 1 P.M.

Is the world going crazy?

I realize this conversation is going in a direction I didn't expect, and she glares at me when I start to laugh. A girl doctor? Who ever heard of such a thing?

But I see how Geri's eyes have gotten squinty, and I immediately change my laugh to an uncontrollable cough. She thumps me on the back, supposedly to help me stop coughing, but we both know she just wants to smack me, and she hits hard for a girl.

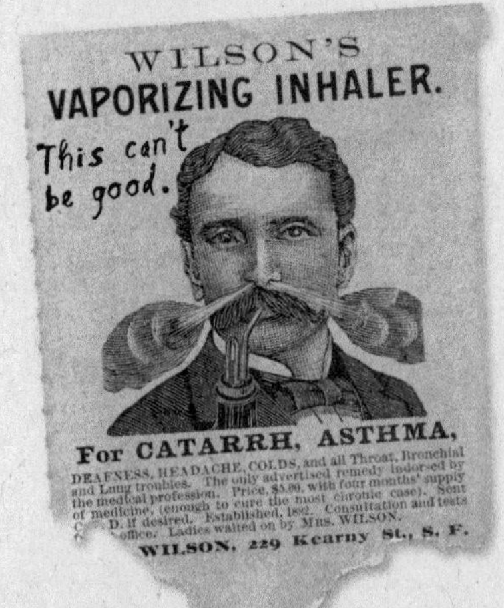

"Hmmm. That cough sounds a bit asthmatic. I might have a cure for that."

I am almost 88.2 percent positive I would rather have asthma, whatever that is, than Geri's "cure," so I immediately stop coughing. "I'm just dandy," I exclaim, choking on another cough. Geri glares at me.

"You might want to reconsider your 'girl' remarks," she says. "For one thing, what about that little girlfriend you have back home? What's her name? Lettie Lou? Sally Sue?"

I feel my jaw tighten. "Lydia Mae," I say, "and she's not my girlfriend. She's barely a girl." I think about her laugh. And her mom's buttermilk biscuits.

"Well," Geri says, "whatever you want to call her, she *is* a girl, and girls will one day rule the world. Who knows, you could need my help one day."

I have no response to such a ridiculous statement. Rule the world? Ha! And I would never need help from a girl.

"Don't think I'm unaware of the low expectations our society has for girls. I simply plan to greatly exceed them and change the way we view women." She gazes off in the distance like she has made a speech to the Congress of Representatives or President Grover Cincinnati himself.

"Cleveland, Stan. It's Grover *Cleveland*."

Details, details. None of that matters as long as it's still part of Ohio.

"It does matter, Stan. It's our president!"

Boy, sometimes it sure is easy to tell Geri and Granny are related.

I simply nod. Uncle Carl says women always get the last word in every fight; otherwise you're just starting a new fight.

Geri sighs and gets down to business. I let her point me toward the building farthest away. "That's the van, where my daddy sells stuff the shanty boys may need. Medicine, tobacco, trousers, those sorts of things. To the left is the barn where the teamsters sleep with their horses."

"In the barn?" I exclaim. I'm genuinely surprised the men have to sleep in the barn with the animals.

"Oh, believe you me, they'd rather sleep in the barn. It's warmer with the horses, and there aren't any lice."

Geri removes her hands from my shoulders and folds her arms across her chest. She is such a swellhead, and it ain't pretty.

"What did you say?" Geri moves toward me, her eyes glaring.

"Huh? Uhhhh, I said, 'Something smells dead, and it might be gritty.' "

She looks at me like I'm a sandwich short of a picnic.

"You don't smell that?" I sniff loudly and look her straight in the eyes like she's the crazy one. "So, what's that building over there?"

Geri guides me around. She tells me the bunkhouse smells like socks, a soggy scent mixed with the grubby stench of fifty men and smoke from the woodstove smoldering in the middle of the room.

She starts listing awful things contained in the bunkhouse. "Cooties jump on you the minute you step inside the door. The shanty boys spit tobacco juice on the stove to try to make it smell better in there. They don't take a bath the whole time they're here. I've seen Jan Jespersen wash his breeches one time in the past three months, and he was the only one. And as I said, there are lice. Lots of them." Geri shudders at the thought. "You do *not* want to spend time in there," she says.

This is a girl who didn't flinch when Conrad McAllister spit at me and it landed on her shoe back in October. A girl who punched Conrad a good one and then held a hankie on his nose until it stopped bleeding. A girl who once cut apart a cockroach just to see how it was put together. She sent me its legs in an envelope with a note that said, "A delicacy in South America!" I think it's one of the only things I haven't saved in my Scrapbook. That envelope went right in the garbage.

So if Geri doesn't want to go in the bunkhouse, it sounds like the perfect spot to escape from her in an emergency. It also sounds like the exact place you would find someone looking for adventure. Someone like my dad. Or me.

CHAPTER 9

"Guess which shanty boy killed a man," Geri whispers.

I immediately look up from stoking the woodstove.

"Hush." Granny's sour breath cuts between us, and she gives Geri her death stare. "Geraldine, you are well aware Stanley has no control over his imagination. Any information like that and he'll conjure up some outlandish fantasy about a murderer on the premises. And we just got over those ridiculous werewolf nightmares." She takes a deep breath and looks me square in the eye. "Don't let your thoughts run away with you, child."

I nod, but truthfully, it's too late. I'm already on the lookout for a killer.

And I'm not a child.

Uncle Henry sidles up to the stove, hugs Aunt Lois, and kisses Geri on the head before stealing a roll. He messes up my hair, winks at me, and puts a finger to his lips. When you're the boss of a place, you can get away with things.

Men trudge into the cook shanty. No one speaks, although a couple of them nod at Uncle Henry. More than one man takes a glance at Mama, she being new and all. They're quieter than I would expect a bunch of rowdy men to be; for some reason, Uncle Henry doesn't allow any conversation, and that kind of strikes me as strange.

"Conversations lead to fistfights," he says as we watch the shanty boys pile in for dinner. Each man takes a spot at the long tables like they've been assigned seats.

"They *have* been assigned seats." Geri snorts. "They're like a bunch of wild animals. Some of them are hiding from the sheriff." Her eyes widen at me. Mine are going to pop out of my head.

Then I see him.

Bushy eyebrows and a grizzled black beard hide the man's probably pockmarked cheeks, and his eyes are so dark you can't see the pupil. A sash, red as blood, is tied around his waist. He's not especially tall, but he's broad like a capital letter T and looks exactly like the man in the Wanted! poster hanging in the post office back home. Except maybe that guy is tall and skinny. And has blond hair. And doesn't have a beard. Other than that, they could be twins.

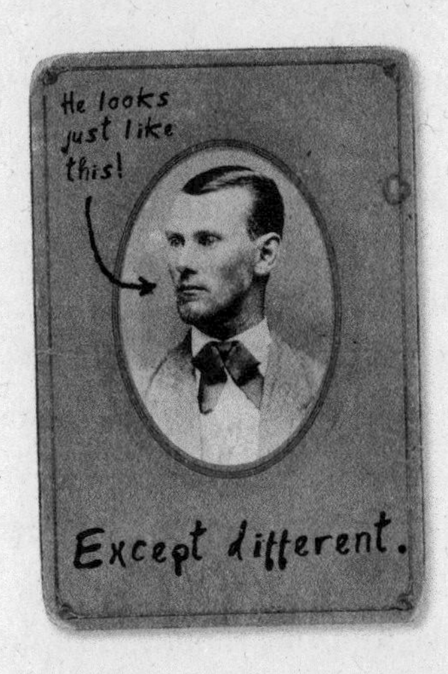

I freeze. I am living with a cold-blooded killer. A man with a heart so black he took the life of another human being. My life is definitely in danger, but I can't stop myself staring at him. Little pieces of food dot his beard. He rubs his eye and stabs some pork with his fork.

Granny nudges me. "Get to work. Those plates are not going to fill themselves," she orders, pointing to the rapidly vanishing food.

Salt pork disappears. Aunt Lois's baked beans are fast becoming a baked bean. Geri runs around filling up mugs as grunts of approval mix with the scraping of plates. I know we have to wait until the lumberjacks are done before we can eat, but I think I might need to hide some food for myself or else it will all be gone. I'm so hungry I could eat a horse and chase the rider.

Hey! Come back here!
I just want to talk!

Instead of food, however, Granny hands me a pail. "Run to the river and bring in some fresh water," she orders.

Making my way through the dark, I hear the men kidding each other as they return to the bunkhouse. So far I've learned that lumberjacks swear, spit, and scratch under their arms, as well as other unmentionable places. It feels like I shouldn't be listening, but if I study these men, manly men who are brave, adventurous, and not afraid of a little danger, maybe I can learn their secrets and stop being just "somewhat" a man.

Also, I feel like someone should warn these guys that if Granny hears their language, she will wash their mouths with soap. And that stuff tastes really bad.

Not that I would know anything about that.

I sneak a glance at the cold-blooded killer, because it is always good to be prepared. He laughs and talks with his friends, pretending he's all innocent, but I know differently.

I will be keeping my eye on him.

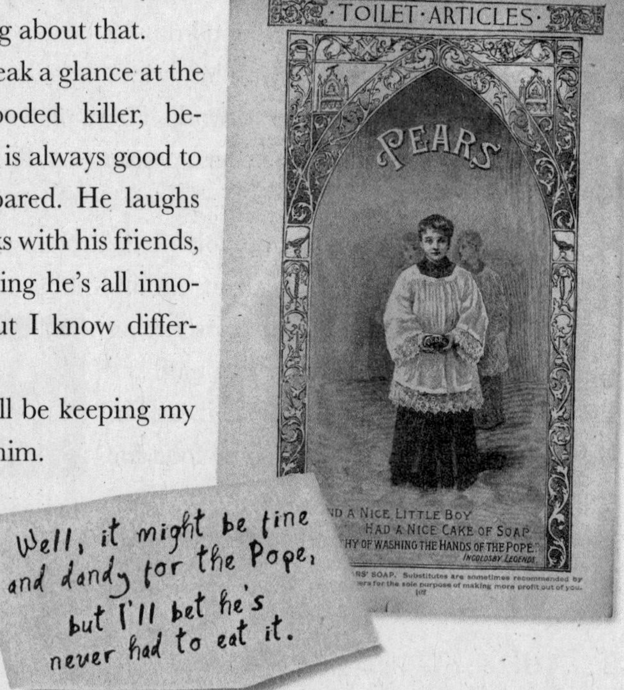

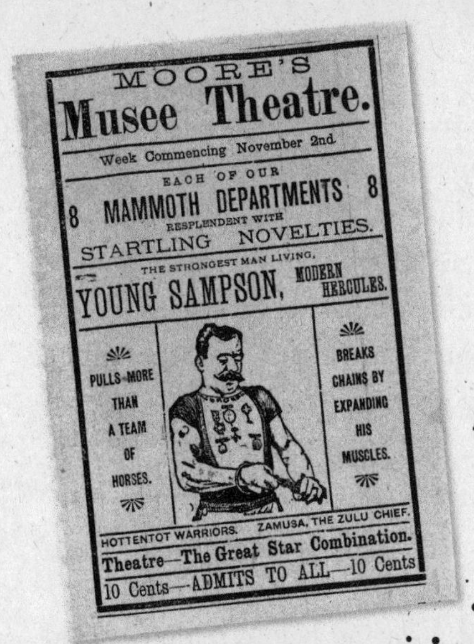

Don't tell anyone, but I'm the tiniest bit afraid of that Granny.

CHAPTER 10

So, Alice," Uncle Henry asks Mama, "what's the plan?" He shovels some baked-bean-soaked bread into his mouth. The table jiggles a little when Aunt Lois kicks Uncle Henry for some reason, and the way she glares at him, I'm pretty sure it wasn't an accident.

"Well, Henry, I'm going to play it by ear, if that's okay with you." Mama looks down at her lap.

"Of course it is, honey," Aunt Lois says, piling meat onto Mama's plate. "You're welcome as long as you want."

I'm focused on getting as much food into my belly as I can. Granny grabs my arm. "Slow down," she orders between her teeth. I glance over at Uncle Henry, cramming food into his craw like it's fixin' to disappear any moment. Granny sees me. "He's a man, Stanley." She smiles sweetly at Uncle Henry. "More beans?"

What is going on? Uncle Henry doesn't need manners. He doesn't answer to Granny. She ignores his swearing, his dirty hands, even his burping at the table. Now that I think about it, she never tells any man what to do.

I need to grow up. Fast.

"Alice, do you think you'll be around for the river drive?" Uncle Henry asks through a mouthful of pork.

"No," Granny says sharply.

Mama's head drops for a second before she lifts it and says, "Well . . ."

"No," Granny repeats. "Taking Stanley on that wanigan, surrounded by those river pigs—hopping on logs, showing off their stupidity with dangerous stunts—it's not the appropriate environment for a young boy. Stan will return to school by the time the ice melts." She looks at me like that's a statement I would agree with. "You'll thank me when you're older," she says to me with a smirk.

Mama glares at Granny, her mouth slightly open, and I see Aunt Lois gently lay a hand on Mama's arm. "I know you want a say in your own child's life, but she has a point, Alice," Aunt Lois says quietly.

Mama nods in reluctant agreement. "I know, I know. I would be a nervous wreck with Stan on that river. It's just that every once in a while it might be nice for Mother to treat me like an adult, not a child."

Aunt Lois smiles sympathetically. "We all know that in regard to academics, Stan is whip smart, but common sense is not his forte, and a wanigan is no place for cavorting."

Did she say "cavorting"? Why, Aunt Lois doesn't know beans about cavorting. As if I would ever cavort.

"Do you even know what that means?" Geri leans over and whispers to me.

"Of course," I reply. "But I'm not going to discuss it in front of the ladies," I add politely.

And what about this "wanigan"? I'm not going to pretend to know what that might be, but it sounds like something I would enjoy. I imagine myself talking to Lydia Mae, telling her what I did while I was gone, how I killed myself a wanigan. Or maybe I tamed one. Or I rode a wanigan like a wild mustang through the woods, carrying a load of green gold to the river, one-handed, while waving an ax.

"You are such a beef-witted apple john." I turn to see Geri shaking her head at me, arms crossed. "A wanigan is the raft we live and cook on during the river drive. What a ninny you are," she says, half to herself, but I can plainly hear her.

"I knew that," I scoff. "I was just seeing if you did." Truth be told, I didn't even know I was thinking out loud. I have to stop doing that.

Geri looks at me skeptically.

"So what was last year's river drive like?" I ask. I pretend to brush dirt off my trousers and try to keep the eagerness out of my voice, when really I'm dying to know the details of such a dangerous and amazing adventure. I can already imagine getting to live and cook while floating on the river—I would practically be Huck Finn.

"Well, Elijah Stewart challenged Harley Garland to a contest to see who could chop a piece of wood the size of a matchstick off a log."

"That's not even possible," I say, rolling my eyes.

"Yes, yes, it is. And they both did it with one swing of an ax."

"Pshaw. I think I could probably do that, too, if Granny would let me have my own ax." I look around nervously. She would immediately dismiss that idea if she heard me, and probably the brain it came from.

"Don't be daft. You couldn't do that. You don't even have the muscles to pick up an ax, let alone swing it over your head."

"Your cheese has slipped off your cracker if you think that, missy," I say. Sometimes I find if I say something like I believe it, it almost becomes true.

"Then why don't you show me?" Geri challenges.

"I, uh, I will! As soon as a spare ax shows up." And Granny is nowhere near. I act like I have all the confidence in the world, but really the thought of picking up an ax makes me as nervous as a long-tailed cat in a room full of rocking chairs. I will be keeping track of any spare axes, just to make sure I hide them before Geri challenges me to a dare I can't ignore. "So what else happened during this river drive?" I say, changing the subject.

"The best thing was when Emil Johnston and Dennie Cheeseman challenged each other to see who could roll a log in the water for the longest period of time," Geri tells me.

This I would love to see. "And?"

"They began at the crack of dawn on a Wednesday and didn't stop rolling until Saturday, when Emil fell in the drink, smashed his leg between two logs, and had to be dragged out with a cant hook. Lost his peavey, too." She shakes her head. "It was a real shame."

"What?" I look around to make sure no one is hearing the language coming from Geri's mouth. Also, I can't for the life of me imagine how much it would hurt to lose your peavey. I cross my legs at the thought. "You kiss your mother with that mouth?"

She peers at me disbelievingly. "What are you talking about?"

I glance around again and lower my voice. "A girl of your background should not be using such a word."

Geri's eyes take on a defiant gleam. "What word? 'Peavey'?"

I gasp. And to think I thought she was a lady.

"Stan," she says, "a peavey is a pole with a sharp spike at the end. It's used to roll and handle logs in the water. What did you think it was?"

I uncross my legs. "That's exactly what I thought."

I'm not even going to get into what a dumb tool a cant hook must be. It apparently can't hook and doesn't have a dangerous point.

So it's of no use to me.

CHAPTER 11

Geri stands. "There's never a dull moment on the river. Too bad you won't be there," she gloats.

I know she doesn't give a hoot that I won't be going on the river drive. I wish beyond wishing I didn't give a hoot, either, but I can't stop myself wishing. "Why do *you* get to go and I can't?" I ask desperately.

Geri looks around, making sure no one is listening. Mama and Aunt Lois are deep in conversation, their foreheads practically touching. Granny has hopped up and started on the dishes, and Uncle Henry has already left. "For a couple of reasons." She sits back down next to me. "First of all, Daddy says I can, and Granny never, ever tells a man what to do, especially when it concerns raising his child. And second, Granny doesn't care what I do."

This is true. Granny hardly pays attention to Geri except to remind her to act like a lady, and it's always been obvious Granny likes boys more than girls, but who wouldn't? And even though I surely don't want her attention, Granny is a lot more protective of me than she is of Geri. But why?

"Because I'm a girl. Sometimes it's better to be a girl," she says smugly.

Now that I think about it, Mama always complains that Granny gives her sons more attention than her daughters. Something about daughters just needing to find a good husband and sons needing to support a family, maybe? Something about sons, and I suppose grandsons, being the future of the family and therefore needing more so they can be strong and competitive?

Maybe it would be easier to be a girl. I rack my brain trying to imagine ways of becoming a girl without actually becoming a girl. The closest I come up with is a picture I once saw in the *Little Lord Fauntleroy* book Mama read to me when I was a little kid.

Somehow I don't think that would go over too well out here.

Geri leans into her chair, so full of herself; if she weighed less, her swelled head could float her up to the ceiling. I have a strong urge to stick a pin in her to deflate the superior look on her face.

And that's when I can't help the words spilling from my mouth. "Well, Granny might leave you alone because you're a girl, but I can be a doctor and you can't!" To be honest, I don't have the teensiest desire to be a doctor. Last I checked they don't even carry anything sharp in their little black bags—though I didn't get much of a look in Dr. Wilson's bag because the one time I had a chance to search it, he walked into the room and almost caught me.

Geri sits up so quickly I'm afraid her chair will crack. "What did you say?" Her eyes are blazing and I can tell I hit a nerve.

"I am simply stating the facts: girls aren't cut out to be doctors. Boys are." I shrug because, hey, I don't make these rules.

Geri shakes a finger at me. "Have you never heard of my hero, Elizabeth Blackwell?"

"You want to be an ax murderer?" I gasp. Also, I'm a little scared. My life might be in serious danger.

Guilty of improper use of ax

The famous rhyme gets trapped in my head: "Lizzie Blackwell took an ax and gave her mother forty whacks." I won't get a lick of sleep tonight. And someone might want to say something to Aunt Lois. We certainly don't need another cold-blooded killer at this lumber camp.

"You are nuttier than a squirrel's cheeks in October. Not Lizzie Borden, you idiot. *Elizabeth Blackwell.*" She says the name slowly, like that will help.

I shake my head and shrug, though I do feel a bit relieved that her hero isn't an ax murderer.

"What? You've never heard of Elizabeth Blackwell?"

Geri exhales, long and slow like her patience with my stupidity is coming rapidly to an end. "She's only the first woman to become a doctor in America," she prods, hoping to jostle my memory.

Really a man

I look at her, my face blank. I vaguely remember Granny mentioning this Blackwell person, but I'm not owning up to it.

"Nope." I shake my head. "Still nothing."

Geri sighs loudly. "And this is why women have trouble advancing in the sciences," she says.

"Or maybe they just aren't created for such academic work," I suggest not so innocently. "Perhaps it's best if the woman stays in the home where she rightfully belongs." I wait for Geri to respond. She's usually as cool as a cucumber, so to see her riled up tickles my funny bone.

I might have smiled a little bit. At the corners of my mouth. You couldn't even see my teeth.

Geri's shoulders hunch, and I can practically see steam coming from her ears like a train barreling down a track. That's when she utters the words that hurt me the most.

"At least I have a father," she snarls, and stomps off.

A shadow seems to pass over the low-lying sun. For years no one has mentioned hide nor hair of my formerly dearly departed father, so I tended not to think about him much. Sure, there were times when it felt like part of me was missing, like I had lost three fingers from my left hand, fingers I'd never used much but wished I still had.

And sure, Mama tries to do everything two parents would do, but to be perfectly honest, she's a girl. Most moms are. And girls don't understand boy stuff like peeing in the snow or the sudden need to jump a fence blindfolded. Moms just shake their heads.

But now, in a matter of weeks, my dad's been like the return of a memory I never knew I had—still fuzzy, but definitely stuck in my brain. He appears like a niggling feeling of doubt right in that twitchy time before I fall asleep, when I close my Scrapbook and shut the envelope tightly between its pages. As much as Mama says I'm the peaches to her cream, I sometimes can't help thinking that my father isn't dead; he just hasn't tried to find me. And I'm not even the one who's lost.

Granny always says you can't miss what you've never had. But you can still *want* what you've never had. I've never had a bicycle, but I long for one like I long for fresh air after a full day stuck in school.

Sometimes wishing for something is worse than missing it.

Unfortunately, as much as I love Mama, she's not enough to get me to the river drive, an event so amazing men are willing to risk their peaveys for a chance to go. For that I need a father. Well, there are fifty men in a bunkhouse next door, and it wouldn't surprise me a bit if one of them is my dad. After all, Granny was very clear: my father may be lost, but he's alive and he could be anywhere. Or, I guess, anyone.

Dear Son,

I am a lumberjack! It is the manliest of professions, and I am quite good at it. Usually I fell about twenty trees a day by myself with just one arm and an ax; then I load them by myself and pull them to the river. By myself. The best thing of all? No girls! Also, no baths, no chores, and no one telling me to use a hankie. Yesterday I spent the afternoon in my bunk reading Huck Finn and picking my nose. And guess what? No one told me not to!

Being a lumberjack is the best. Now, don't get me wrong. It's hard work! You need muscles and brains and lots of hair on your chest to be a lumberjack.

When you find me, I will be sure to let your granny know you can go on that river drive. You can jump on logs with me and ride them down the river while people wave from shore. We'll call your cousin Scary Geri, climb a tree so she can't catch us, and then drop pinecones on her head.

And if I find you first, I will give you your very own peavey and never ever make you clean behind your ears. You can grow potatoes back there for all I care.

From,
Your Dad

Who's to say he's not a lumberjack?

Oh, how I miss you, indoor water closet!

CHAPTER 12

I grab my plate and Geri's. I finish her potatoes.

Waste not, want not.

"Get over here and help dry the dishes," Granny barks. Everyone except Geri pitches in. We clean the kitchen and the dishes and sweep the floors and I'm plain tuckered out. I don't know how I will ever get up and go chop trees in the morning, but a man's gotta do what a man's gotta do.

Granny, Mama, and I stagger into our room. It's cold, even though the woodstove is hot when you touch it.

I stick the tip of my finger in my mouth. It still hurts.

I open the door to the outside and wind whips my face with tiny, hard pellets of snow. I'm not going to trudge to the outhouse in this weather. I look behind me and see Granny occupied at the washbasin. Mama is behind the curtain, changing into her nightclothes.

Naturally this is the perfect opportunity to pee out the door. I'm at a lumber camp. This is how we men do things here.

"No, we do *not*." Granny grabs my ear and twists it.

"Do you not see that I'm busy here, missy?" I yelp.

"Oh, I certainly do see that you're busy." She twists my ear again for good measure. Or simply because she's evil. "This will *not* happen again. You see that over there?" She points through the night to a building neither of us can see in the dark, swirly snow. "That's the outhouse. Otherwise known as the 'necessary' or 'privy.' I don't care what you call it; just use it. We aren't animals."

I nod, button up my trousers, and try not to catch her eye, then splash my face with the water in the washbasin. My woolen underdrawers aren't very warm, but they'll have to do under the pile of blankets.

I pull down the covers, heave myself quickly into bed, and snuggle in. Except I can't actually snuggle in too far. It's like my feet are trapped midway to the bottom of the bed, the blanket stopping them like a wall.

"What in the Sam Hill?" I mumble as I try again to jam my feet under the covers.

"Stanley Slater! Did I hear you reference the devil himself?" Granny roars.

"Uh, no, Granny," I respond, thinking quickly while

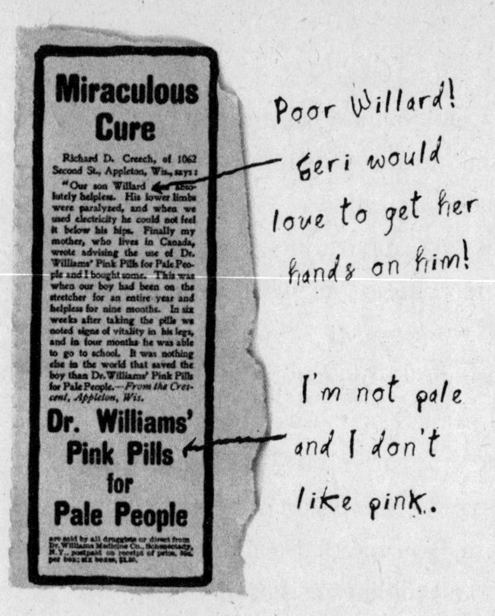

Miraculous Cure

Richard D. Creech, of 1062 Second St., Appleton, Wis., says:

"Our son Willard [illegible] absolutely helpless. His lower limbs were paralyzed, and when we used electricity he could not feel it below his hips. Finally my mother, who lives in Canada, wrote advising the use of Dr. Williams' Pink Pills for Pale People and I bought some. This was when our boy had been on the stretcher for an entire year and helpless for nine months. In six weeks after taking the pills we noted signs of vitality in his legs, and in four months he was able to go to school. It was nothing else in the world that saved the boy than Dr. Williams' Pink Pills for Pale People.—*From the Crescent, Appleton, Wis.*

Dr. Williams' Pink Pills for Pale People

are sold by all druggists or direct from Dr. Williams Medicine Co., Schenectady, N.Y., postpaid on receipt of price, 50c. per box; six boxes, $2.50.

trying to get safely beneath the blankets. "I just wondered if, um, you had a pain pill."

"Are you feeling all right?" Mama peers over the railing with concern. I have my knees pulled to my chest and am trying to force them toward the bottom of the bunk with no luck.

"Yes. I'm. Fine," I mutter. Mama surveys the scene, trying not to smile, but the corner of her mouth turns up like a fish caught on a lure. Except she's obviously enjoying herself a whole lot more.

"Um, I think someone has short-sheeted your bed, honey," she says, peeling back the blankets. Sure enough, the bottom one has been folded in half so every time I try to draw the blanket over me while pushing down with my feet, I'm basically folding myself into a pasty.

"Geri," I say with a scowl.

Mama's eyes dart to Granny. "I do believe your granny was correct when she said you won't be bored here." She fixes my bed and tucks me in. "Say your prayers," she reminds me with a kiss.

Now I lay me down to sleep
I pray the Lord my soul to keep
If I should die before I wake
I pray the Lord my soul to take.

This is not my favorite prayer because it gives me the jimjams. I have a hard enough time getting to sleep thinking about loups-garous, ways to outwit Granny and Geri, and finding my father, so this prayer doesn't help. I don't like to think I might die before I wake; that idea kind of makes me not want to go to sleep, just in case.

"Alice, did I just hear the boy say he doesn't like to pray? I fear for his very soul. Let me out so I can box his ears." The bunk jiggles a bit and I curl myself all the way under the blankets so that Granny's pinchy fingers can't reach me.

Mama murmurs something soothing as I drift off to sleep, and I say a little prayer of thanks that Mama and Granny share a bed and Granny is next to the wall.

Distantly I hear Granny mutter that I'm sure to turn into a bad egg. Or did she say she's shipping me off to Winnipeg? Or cutting off my one good leg?

I'm so tired, I honestly don't care.

CHAPTER 13

Sure enough, when I wake up, I'm dead.

The horn of the angel Gabriel himself has called me home to Heaven. It's so loud, I jerk awake and almost knock my head on the beam above me, although it probably wouldn't hurt, seeing as I'm dead and all.

A soft whistle might be nice when called to Heaven. Or a warm breeze and a hug from Mama. This horn business is too dad-blamed loud. Who wants to be called to Heaven like Conrad McAllister has slugged you in the face?

"Roll out the dead bodies, daylight in the swamp!" someone yells.

It's not just me. We're all dead. This day is not starting off so well.

Half-asleep, I yank up my wool pants and tuck them into my socks. The bite in the air surprises me; I guess I thought Heaven wouldn't make my nose all cold and drippy. I wipe it off with my sleeve, which I've learned is a manly thing to do, and realize that if it were too hot in here, I would probably need to worry about my very soul. I push open the door to the kitchen, ready to meet my maker.

Unfortunately, the first thing I see is Granny. And then I know.

This ain't Heaven.

"Gabriel horn wake you?" Uncle Henry asks, stuffing bacon into his mouth.

What is it with this family and bacon?

"How did you know? Did you hear it, too?"

"Hear it? Why, I blew it!" Uncle Henry declares.

Uncle Henry is the angel Gabriel. Who would have thought? This information certainly would have come in handy when I was alive. Especially when it was time to take a test, or the last time Conrad McAllister threatened to beat me up; he thought I had called him a "dizzy-eyed barnacle," when the truth is . . . Well, that is the truth. I did call him a "dizzy-eyed barnacle." That's no reason to beat someone up, though. Good thing I can run fast and Conrad is not exactly skin and bones.

Uncle Henry laughs, a deep, hearty laugh that sounds

like Aunt Lois's homemade noodles smothered in real butter. He throws an arm around my shoulders and gives me a hard squeeze.

"It's just a Gabriel horn, son. It's what you'll hear every morning around this time to wake up the shanty boys, get them fed, and send them off to work."

"Stan, grab these flapjacks and put them on the table." Aunt Lois hands me a plate loaded with more flapjacks than I have eaten in my entire life. Fried potatoes, sowbelly, baked beans, some molasses syrup, and pork sausages weigh down the table.

I'm hungry, but when you think you're dead and you suddenly find out you're not, it takes a minute to sink in and can really affect your appetite. I hope I don't lose my ability to eat altogether, or I'm sure to waste away to nothing.

Men shuffle in. Some pull up suspenders, and others tie red sashes around their waists. One of the men says something to Mama. No, make that two of the men say something to Mama. She smiles a little from behind the stove and her cheeks turn a pretty pink.

I'm not sure I like it.

I survey the scene, searching for someone who might be my father. I see a guy with a beard. And there's another guy with a beard. And a guy with a really bushy beard. And a guy with so much facial hair, I swear he has a beard growing on top of his beard. I'm pretty sure my father's own mother wouldn't be able to pick him out of this crowd; they all look so much alike, it's apparent I need to come up with another plan.

I grab the teapot and start pouring; then I spy an empty seat and quietly slip into it.

I might have spilled some syrup and knocked over a couple of plates, but other than that I was really quite quiet.

"Hello, son," the man on my left says, elbowing me lightly.

I look at him and realize with a shock that he's the guy Geri said was a cold-blooded killer. He nods at me. "Name's Peter," he says, his mouth full of food. Not only has he killed a man, he has a pathetic name for a criminal, and horrible manners to boot.

I point at his chest. "I'm onto you, Stinky Pete," I say.

Only I say this in my head. And I don't actually point at his chest with my finger, but I do stare at it really hard. He knows that I know, and he is afraid. Or maybe I am.

I turn to my right. "Hi," I whisper. I know there's no talking, but finding my father and getting myself to the river drive are more important than that harebrained rule. Eyes peer at me from above lifted forks. It appears "No Talking" is taken very seriously. Then I notice Granny heading in my direction; I have to be quick.

"Does the name Stanley Slater mean anything to you?" I hiss to the man next to me.

"Are you Mrs. Slater's son?" the guy asks.

"Yes! Yes, I am!" First try and I've found my father. "You know her?"

"Since yesterday. We all know her, boy. She's the only woman to set foot on this property since we arrived in October. Not counting Lois, of course. She's off-limits."

This is sounding much less promising.

"I'm Stan, by the way."

"Cager."

It's pretty clear he's not my father, but if I were going to change my name, that's the exact name I would choose.

Men start pushing themselves away from the table. Some pull their bright wool socks up over their trousers or retie their leather boots. Cager nods to me and starts to get up, which is okay because Granny is trying to maneuver her way through the shanty boys to get to me—a clear sign that I need to go in the opposite direction. Fast.

"Give a good word to your ma for me." I think Cager is smiling, but it's hard to tell under all the hair.

I freeze when two hands land on my shoulders. Scratchy hair tickles my cheek.

"Put in a good word for me, too, eh?" My heart drops to my shoes when I look into the sinister, twinkly eyes of Stinky Pete, cold-blooded killer. He lightly squeezes my shoulders and gently pats my head—a warning of things to come, I'm sure. And what happens next only confirms my suspicions.

"Hey, if you're up for it, I'd be happy to play you in a game of cribbage later," he says with a grin.

"Watch out for that guy," Cager says. "He will murder you at card games."

I knew it! I am a whiz at first impressions, I don't mind saying. Even when they're more like second impressions.

Stinky Pete winks at me, then ominously whistles his way into the dark.

He should probably keep walking straight out of the lumber camp, because there ain't no way I'm letting a dangerous man like him near my mama.

CHAPTER 14

"What was that all about?" Granny's arms are crossed in front of her chest. "You've been carrying on like an old biddy."

Which is hardly fair.

I don't look anything like an old biddy.

I squint at Granny. Her eyes are worse than I thought. "How many fingers am I holding up?"

She squints at me. "Two. Why?"

"Hmmm. Just checking your eyesight." It appears to be okay, although she might have simply had a lucky guess. "Have to go eat now. Great chat, Granny!" I pat her arm and run off to the stove to finally fill up my plate.

"What were you talking about with the boys?" Granny murmurs into my ear. That woman is fast for her age. She's got to be forty-five years old if she's a day. I look around for someone to save me, but they've all plopped themselves down to eat.

I see how things are here; it's every man for himself.

"Well"—I take a deep breath—"if you really must know, they were asking me about Mama."

Granny perks up and looks around like she's lost all the pieces of a puzzle and they're scattered about this room. "Yes. This is a perfect place to find exactly what Alice needs," she mutters to herself. "Why didn't I think of that? Alice needs a reliable man around, and where better to find a man but a lumber camp filled with them?"

She grabs her plate and marches over to the table.

I'm a little in shock. On the one hand, Hey! I didn't get in trouble! On the other hand, What does she mean, "Alice needs a reliable man around"?

I sit down to eat, thoughts swirling around my brain. Somehow I think my plan for adding a man to the family is a bit different from Granny's—I'm just planning on adding the one who already belongs. And if I can't manage that, I'm simply going to have to become a man myself. Fast.

Geri passes me the sugar. I pour it into my tea and take a giant gulp.

"Pffft!" It isn't sugar. Someone put salt in the sugar bowl.

Geri is bent in half, laughing. Granny mutters something about wasting food, a tiny smile curling her lip. I'm so mad, I pick up my plate and head to my room.

I don't need these people. I'll just eat by myself.

Mama comes up behind me. "Don't pay them no never mind," she says. Her voice is smooth and calm, and her eyes are as clear blue as Lake Superior two days after the ice melts.

"Mama, I'm going to kill that tickle-brained pumpion," I sputter. "She is plain off her chump."

Mama rubs my back. "Well, honey, you don't know for certain that Geri pulled that little prank."

I look at her like she's got mush for brains.

"Honestly, pranks in lumber camps are hardly unusual," she says. "Last year when Granny was helping Lois at the camp in Grand Marais, they told me about a prank that left a shanty boy bald and headfirst in a snowbank." She winks at me. "He was new and apparently had criticized Granny's biscuits after spitting tobacco juice on her clean floor." We both nod knowingly. That was not a good idea. "Also, if it *is* Geri, you don't want to give her the satisfaction of knowing it bothers you."

I know this trick. I know it's just a way to make sure there's not an all-out prank war between us, but I'm not sure I'm sold on the reasoning.

"Oh, grow up," Granny says from the doorway. "Don't be such a mama's boy. Now finish up and get in here and help us clean. We don't have all day. And don't even think of trying to get back at Geri. That girl has more bad thoughts in her head than Attila the Hun. If you try to out-prank her, I can pretty much guarantee you'll be cooking your own goose."

I shake my head, because as much as I hate to admit it, the old biddy has a point.

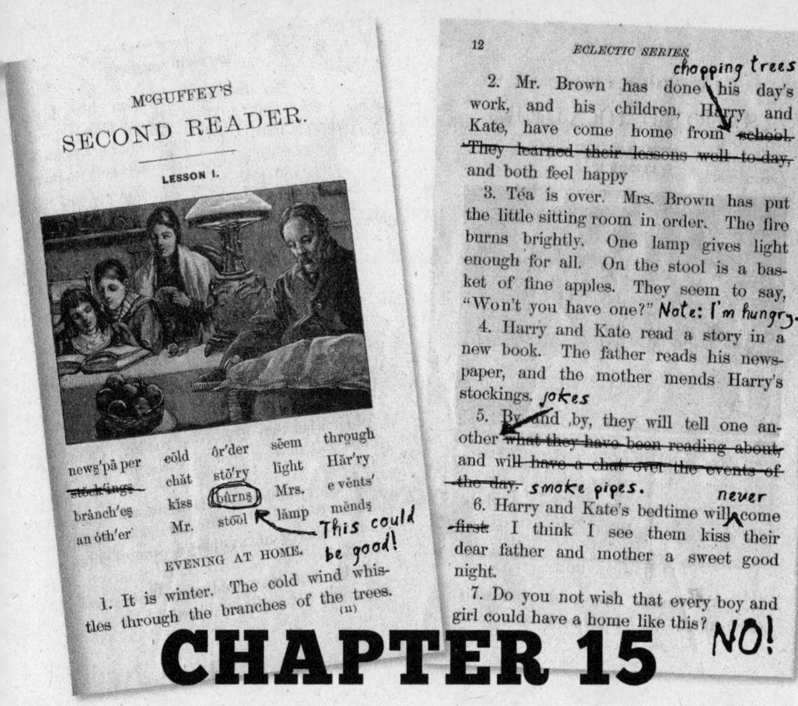

CHAPTER 15

I have been swindled. Hoodwinked. Bamboozled. After waking up dead, the disappointment of not finding my father yet, a face-to-face conversation with a cold-blooded killer, salt in my tea, and being told I am this close to being a dead duck, the worst thing of all happens.

Granny makes me go to school.

Technically, she brings school to me, but it's the same thing, except I don't have any friends around. Unless you count Geri, and we all know Geri is not my friend.

"Focus on the material, Stanley," Granny drones. I try, but I'm as bored as a pacifist's pistol.

"I am no longer Stanley," I announce. "From now on I will be referred to as Bat."

Geri looks up over her tea and snorts. "Like the mammal?"

"No," I answer. "It's a nickname. We men like our nicknames, because they make us sound tough." Do I have to explain everything to these people?

Not this kind of bat!

"What's it short for? 'Bats in the belfry'?"

"Ha. Ha. Ha." I might have to pick another nickname.

"Stanley. Focus. Read this portion aloud." Granny points to a section in the McGuffey Reader and proceeds to pace behind me while everyone else preps dinner in the kitchen.

"On the stool is a basket of fine apples. They seem to say, 'Won't you have one?'" I pause. Why, if you were an apple, would you invite someone to eat you? Although the talking apple is interesting, I'm just not sure what I'm supposed to learn from this.

"Continue," Granny orders. I read about the Brown family. These people have the worst lives of anyone I've ever encountered in all my livelong days. Apparently the dad comes home from work and reads by himself. The kids come home from school and read by themselves. Mrs. Brown mends some socks. They go to bed. Not one of them even mentions an ax.

I would rather drink a cup of salt than spend an evening with the Brown family.

Geri sits across from me. She looks overly cheerful. She doesn't have to do any of this, but Granny lets her sit and watch and listen.

"Perhaps a little education will rub off," Granny says before heading back to knead her dough.

Geri groans. Not out loud, but her eyes very clearly roll back in her head. She's reading *Home and Health and Home Economics*. I think she stole it from the library.

Geri laughs, which makes me realize two things: (a) I spoke out loud. Again. And (2) she is completely guilty of the act of thievery.

"You know it's legal to borrow books from the library, right, Stan? That's the whole reason behind the library?" she snipes.

"Yes," I reply, "but you're not allowed to keep them forever." I point at her. "You, missy, are going to jail."

Geri shrugs and returns to her reading; then her head snaps up and she looks at me intently. "Hmmm." She tilts her head to the right. She looks down at her book and then quickly at me.

"What?"

"Oh, nothing."

There's nothing that means less than nothing than when someone says "Oh, nothing."

"That makes no sense."

But she knows what I mean.

"It's just . . ." She bends closer to inspect my face.

"What?" I hiss. I am onto her little shenanigans.

She leans back into her chair and nods like she agrees with herself. "Yep. I think you have quinsy."

I just look at her. I'm not falling for this again, especially so soon after the yellow fever scare. I feel perfectly fine, but I can't help wondering, what exactly is quinsy?

"Or it could be a rare, deadly case of spontaneous combustion."

After being awakened by the angel Gabriel himself, you'd think I'd be used to the idea of death, but new ways of dying seem to keep rearing their ugly heads the minute I start to enjoy living. And even though I don't exactly trust Geri, when I think about it, I guess I do feel a bit under the weather. My throat is dry; my eyelids feel sweaty. I loosen my collar so I can breathe.

Geri looks more concerned than devious, so I'm not so sure she isn't telling the truth. "Either one will mean no river drive for you, no matter who says you can go." She seems almost sad, so I decide it's better to be safe than sorry.

"Well, what can we do about it?" I ask, trying not to sound desperate.

"Gee whiz," Geri swears. "Don't get all in a dither." She eats some bacon she pulls out of her pocket.

"I am dying here," I hiss.

"What's the commotion? And why aren't you reading, Stanley?" Granny returns from kneading bread, smelling all warm and yeasty. I like that smell so much, I immediately change her Evil Rating to 95.5 percent.

I know it's a ridiculous reason to change your opinion of someone, but I'm hungry.

"I'm dying, Granny, if you must know. And if I'm nearly

dead, the last thing I want to do is read about some strange family and their holey socks."

"Not again," Granny says. "Geraldine, do you have anything to do with this by chance?"

Geri's eyes get wide. "Why, Granny, how could I? What do I know? I'm just a girl."

"I have quinsy. Or spontaneous combustion. We're not sure which." I look pleadingly at my grandmother. Maybe, for once, she can actually do something useful.

"Child, does your throat hurt?" She places her palm against my forehead. I shake my head.

"And is your body on fire? Perhaps somewhere I can't see?"

I shake my head again. That certainly is an odd question. I'm starting to wonder about her mental ability.

"First of all, quinsy requires a sore throat and a fever, neither of which you have. Second, spontaneous combustion would mean you would suddenly go up in flames for no reason at all, leaving nothing behind but

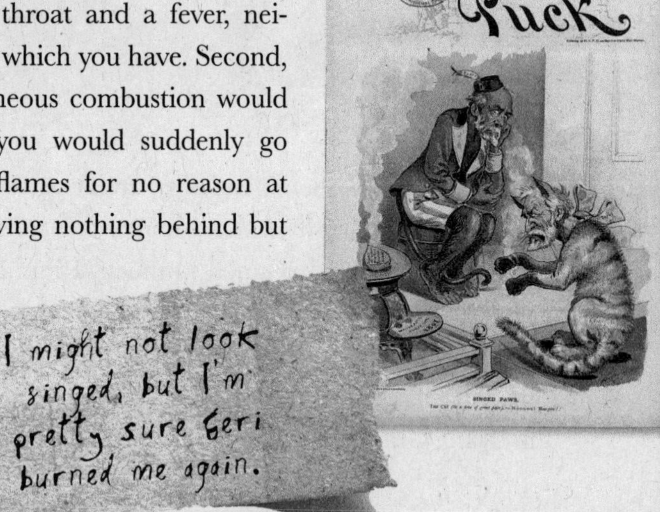

a pile of ashes." She looks me over, head to toe. "I see no evidence of this. You don't even appear to be singed."

Geri smirks through a mouthful of bacon.

"Geraldine, why don't you go help your mother get the boys' lunches together." Granny hands me a cookie. Evil Rating is now 92.2 percent. Someday, a long time from now, I might actually even like her.

"For someone so smart, you can be so gullible," Granny scolds. "Now read. No more distractions." Then she twists my ear, pushes my head toward the book, and stomps into the kitchen.

I definitely spoke too soon.

Just looking at this makes me queasy.

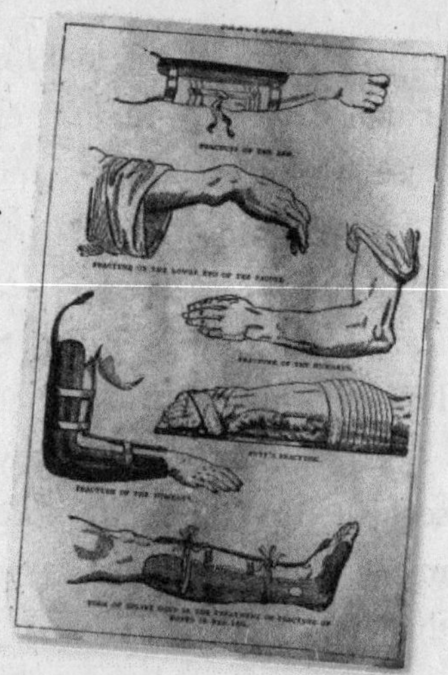

CHAPTER 16

After lunch, I meander into the kitchen to find myself a snack, when lo and behold, I find Geri up to her elbow in a raw chicken.

“What in the dickens are you doing?” I ask, shocked.

She flails her arm around, and the headless, featherless bird bobs up and down like a strange sort of puppet.

“What does it look like I’m doing?” she asks crossly.

I jump back a little so uncooked poultry doesn’t hit me. That would be a difficult bruise to explain. “Well, if you must know, it looks like you have a chicken for a hand puppet.”

“Ugh!” Geri flaps her arm and the dead bird on the counter.

"If it makes you feel any better," I add encouragingly, "I think you're onto something. People would pay good money to see a dead chicken puppet show."

"I am *not* putting on a puppet show! I'm practicing my medicine!"

I notice the needle and thread in her left hand pulling tiny stitches through the bird's skin.

"You're sewing a chicken?" I'm not ashamed to admit I'm more than a little confused. And worried.

"No," Geri says, peering into my face and stretching the word like I'm four quarters short of a dollar. She's got a lot of nerve, considering what she is presently wearing on her arm. "I'm practicing my stitches and setting a broken leg." She finishes her stitch, quickly knots it, and picks up the chicken to admire her handiwork.

Although I will never tell Geri, I am impressed. Not everyone can sew up a hole in a chicken.

"Thank you." She looks pleased.

Then she grabs the drumstick in both hands and snaps it in half. It's enough to make me want to sit down. In the other room.

She is violent.

"There," she says in a satisfied voice. She grabs a knife and some string, straightens the leg, ties the knife to the broken drumstick, and stands back proudly to survey her handiwork.

"Not bad," I say.

Geri's head swings around so fast it might fly off her neck and land in the sink. "Not bad? You're kidding, right? I stitched up that chicken and set its broken leg in less time than it takes you to tie your boots."

"And just in time for dinner," I reply. Whether the chicken has stitches or a broken leg won't matter a wooden nickel in about two hours and forty-three minutes, because we will have eaten it.

"Oh, what do you know. Now help me peel the potatoes." I reach for a peeler and a spud, but Geri slaps my hand for no good reason before I can get close to either one.

"Wash your hands before you touch anything," she orders.

"Why? They don't even look very dirty," I argue.

"Didn't I just see you pick your nose?" Geri accuses me.

"Wha . . . ? What are you talking about?" I stuff my hands in my pockets while Geri looks at me out of the corner of her eye.

"Why in tarnation"—I glance around quickly, making sure Granny isn't lurking somewhere—"would I need to wash my hands?"

She sighs. "It is well known in educated medical circles that washing hands prevents disease. Dr. Oliver Wendell Holmes himself recommended it years ago. Louis Pasteur believes it stops the spread of germs." She waits for my reaction.

All I can do is shrug.

"Boogers carry germs. Germs make you sick."

This coming from someone who carries bacon in her pocket and had a dead bird on her hand.

"That's different." Geri snorts as she slams the chicken into my gut and stomps off. And, of course, this is the exact time Granny chooses to enter the kitchen.

"Stanley Arthur Slater! In all my born days! What are you doing with that chicken? That's dinner, not a toy! Wasting food is not an option unless you want fifty hungry lumberjacks on your hide!" She goes on and on about my lack of responsibility and disregard for the value of money and good food.

Once again, I'm left holding the bag, or in this case, the chicken, and blamed for something I did not do, and Geri gets off free and easy.

Women.

CHAPTER 17

At dinner, I find my father. It sure took long enough. First of all, I've been so busy these last two weeks beating Stinky Pete at cribbage every night, I've almost forgotten to look. I also beat him at euchre, hearts, and one hand of poker when Granny wasn't looking. He makes me a little nervous, however, when he points his finger at me like a gun, winks, and says he'll get me tomorrow. Maybe it's not such a good idea to beat a cold-blooded killer at card games.

Also, my plan to prove my manliness, and thereby prove my ability to help on the river drive, has been greatly hampered by Mama's insistence that I wear an apron at all times in the kitchen. And it just so happens the only apron in my size has large red flowers on it, so my Man Plan is on the back burner. Just until I lose that apron.

In the meantime, I had to shake Granny off my tail so that I could sit down and talk to some of the shanty boys, one of whom I'm sure is my father. I do not have a minute to waste. Uncle Henry keeps a close eye on the weather and the amount of board feet piling up on the roll-aways near the river, so that river drive is happening with or without me. I'm planning on with.

And today I realize, now that I've had the chance to ask some investigative questions, that my father is obviously Knut Knutson: he likes both bacon and me, not necessarily in that order, and he's always slapping my back and telling me bad jokes. Yesterday's joke was "Vat time is it ven an elephant sits on a fence? Time to buy a new fence!" Then he laughed and I laughed. At that time I suspected he might be my father—a good sense of humor could very well run in our family.

But when he walked in today whistling, I knew for sure.

I myself am a whiz at whistling, I don't mind saying. It must be a family talent.

Also, he was the first lumberjack to walk in, and my time is short.

I squeeze in between Cager and Knut to tell him the good news.

"Hey, Knut," I say. "Good news! You are my father."

He is so glad to hear the news he chokes on his ham. "Uh, Stan," he says, "I joost met ya two veeks ago."

"Um, so?" I reply.

"I cannot possibly be yer far."

I look at him squinty-eyed. "Well," I say, "you are."

Knut grins his toothy grin because that's how happy he is to hear he has a son.

Stinky Pete elbows him from the right. "Congrats, old man! It's a boy!" He sniggers. I've got my eye on him. He killed a man.

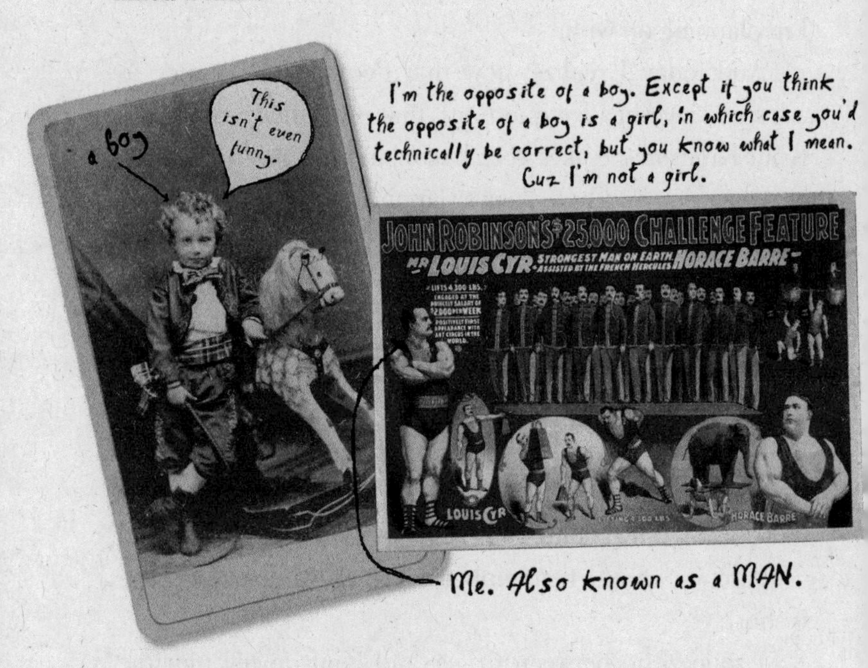

"I vood love to be yer far, but . . ."

"Should I call you that?" I interrupt. "Should I call you 'far'?" I try the strange word on my tongue. "It's not proper English, you know. Well, it's pretty much not English at all, but I am a whiz at other languages, I don't mind saying. I speak Canadian like I was born there."

"But," Knut continues, waving his fork for emphasis, "it cannot be possible."

"Uh, yeah, it is. You have blue eyes and you whistle just like me."

"Yah," he agrees.

"You do have blue eyes, Knut." Stinky Pete nods solemnly. "And I've heard you whistle."

I lean around Knut to face Stinky Pete. "I've got my eye on you, Stinky Pete," I hiss as he draws back from fright.

"Who is Stinky Pete?" he asks, looking confused. He acts so innocent, but he knows that I know that he knows that I know he killed a man.

Now I'm confused, too, so I turn my attention back to Knut.

"Well, Knut, as I said, I have blue eyes like you. And you have a nose . . ." I wait for this to sink in.

"Well, true . . ."

"Me too! And you . . ."

But he rudely interrupts me. "Vat year ver ya born, lad?"

I eye him suspiciously. "It's not polite to ask a lady her age."

"Ya do know yer not a lady, eh?" I nod. "Vat year, den?"

"Eighteen eighty-three," I reluctantly reply.

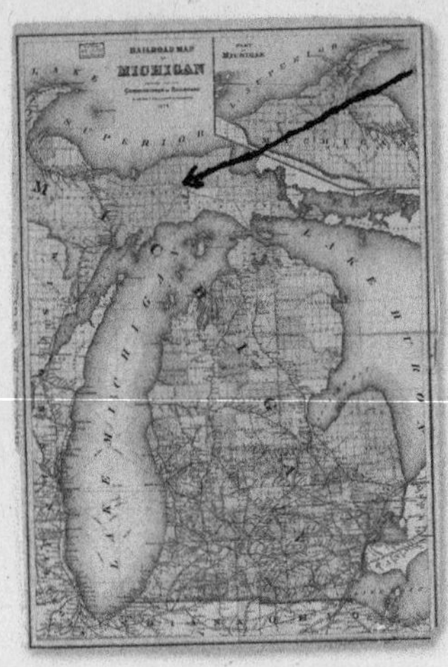

We are here.

Knut pounds the table. "Ya see! I didn't even get ta Mitchigan till eighty-nine! You ver six!"

"I can do math," I say, suddenly feeling quite irritated.

Knut's voice softens. It sounds like butter on corn bread, so it's not so easy to get mad at him.

Also, I like butter. And corn bread. And I'm hungry.

"If'n I ever haf a son, I'd be lucky if'n he vas like you." Knut pats my knee with a little comma of a smile.

I return to my room and pull out my Scrapbook. The envelope is still in there, still empty, still full of secrets. What was my father doing in Texas? I sit down, envelope in front of me, and imagine how great my father probably is—my real father, not some silly but nice guy who tells bad jokes.

I imagine he's out in the world doing something amazing, like mining gold or riding through the Wild West on horseback.

Dear Son,

I'm so glad you liked the nuggets of gold I sent you. Please hide them and don't show them to anyone even if they ask. Especially Geri.

I am headed to Colorado to become a cowboy. I will send you a horse and gun for your birthday, but don't tell anyone so it can be a surprise. And if you tell Geri, make her swear on the library book she stole. Even though that book is dumb.

I miss you very, very much and will write you again soon.

From,
Dad
aka Chicken McPhee

I casually walk to the kitchen to show my letter to Geri, who is standing on a chair, hanging up wet dish towels. This is just the thing to prove to her I have a dad, too.

"Look!" I say. "Look at the letter from my dad! Who misses me and is a gold miner cowboy!"

She climbs down, hands me a damp towel, and takes the paper. "Hmmm," she says jealously. She looks from the letter to me and back to the letter. Her eyebrows squeeze together so tightly, it looks like two hairy caterpillars are having a conversation on her forehead.

"How do I know this is really from your dad?"

I can't believe she would doubt me! I make a shocked face.

Mama looks at me with concern as she sweeps the floor around us. "Are you feeling okay, Stan?"

Apparently I need to work on my shocked face.

"Well? How do I know this is from your dad?" Geri repeats.

"Here's a picture!" I shove a photo at her.

"It looks like someone cut this out of a magazine," she says as she flips it over. I quickly snatch it away.

"Look!" I point to the spot signed "Dad."

Geri looks a little confused. Then her face clears and she nods.

"Oh! Well!" She pauses, obviously trying to get her jealousy under control. "Um."

She clearly needs more time to think about all of this, and I agree—my dad is pretty impressive, even if he does appear to have been cut out of a magazine.

"I'm glad he's doing so well," she says; then she gets a strange, sad look and leaves the room.

She is going to have to face the facts: Uncle Henry is good-natured, trustworthy, reliable, and all, but my dad is a lot more interesting than her dad.

However, he just might be a lot harder to find.

CHAPTER 18

Granny has me scrubbing pots again. Scrubbing pots is the opposite of adventurous, dangerous, and manly, even if the bottom of the pot has oatmeal stuck to it like it's hanging on for dear life.

This is my reality, my adventurous, dangerous, manly reality. And it's been the same thing, day in and day out, for more than a month now. I've already checked all the shanty boys for a sign of my dad, with no luck. Well, all the shanty boys but Cooter the blacksmith, who is older than Methuselah, and Stinky Pete. He can't be my father because he's a cold-blooded killer. He also stinks at cribbage, always wants to talk to me about my day, and helps me get wood for the stove.

He might have other people fooled, but I wasn't born yesterday.

And no matter what I do, I can't seem to get rid of that darn flowered apron. I tucked it behind the woodstove in the kitchen, but Aunt Lois screeched and grabbed it when it started smoking. It was only a little scorched; it's not like it would have started the whole building on fire. So now I'm wearing a flowered apron that is singed on the bottom and smells like smoke even though Mama washed it twice.

I shrugged when she asked me how it got behind the stove. I shrugged when she asked me how it ended up on the road, too. Jan Jespersen, the camp's road monkey, almost ran it over with the ice truck.

THE MONKEYS.

I pretty much have resigned myself to a life in the kitchen in a flowered apron followed by school lessons with Granny and medical advice from Geri. I might be turning into a girl.

So imagine my surprise when Uncle Henry comes up behind me with a man-to-man thump on my shoulder and says, "C'mon, Stan. We're headin' to the woods."

Finally, someone understands I'm meant for more than this toilsome drudgery.

Truth be told, I'm more of a hermit. A quiet soul, one led to chopping wood, whittling twig animals, playing the harmonica to the deer outside my cabin window . . .

"What in the world are you talking about?" Geri looks at me all catawampus from behind her broom. "You have not shut up since you got here. Plus, if you want to get out to those woods with my daddy, you'd better tuck in your pants and tie on that scarf. He's halfway gone and it's colder than a polar bear's toenail outside."

She's right, although I will never utter those words aloud.

"I usually am," Geri agrees.

That is the last time I will utter those words aloud.

I jam my pants into my socks, tie up my boots, pull my hat over my ears, button my coat, and smirk at Granny, leaving the oatmeal-crusted pot soaking in the sink.

"You heard him, woman." I nod at her. "We men are headed to the woods. To do man's work. Which also means I won't be able to finish cleaning that pot," I add with a sad shake of my head.

"Fine by me. It's about time you did some work around

here. But better grab those food pails and load them on the lunch sleigh," Granny orders. "The lumberjacks are not going to be happy to see you if you're empty-handed."

That's when I notice the pails of food heaped by the door. I fail to notice, however, an ax, a saw, or anything remotely sharp. This makes me feel a little relieved, in a strange way. Not that I wouldn't jump at the chance to show my know-how with an ax, I just prefer to do it on my own terms, not because of some stupid dare from Geri.

"Go on. Get going, Mr. Big Man," Granny says, shooing me off with a flick of her wrist. "Oh, and the pot will still be here when you get back."

I glare at that woman while loading up my arms with lunch buckets, then head into the deep winter, the door slamming behind me.

"So, what do you think about camp?" I turn around to see Uncle Henry leaning against the wall and picking his teeth with a whittled twig.

"I think the shanty boys eat too much and I don't eat near enough," I answer, dumping the buckets onto the sleigh.

Uncle Henry snorts. "Oh, those men work so hard and so long, there's not enough food in the world to fill them up." He tosses his twig on the ground and helps me grab another load from the kitchen.

"By the way, have I told you how nice it is to have another man around here? In the cook shanty, I mean," Uncle

Henry says. "Obviously we have enough men on the premises. But those women . . ." He gives me a knowing smile as we load the last of the pails and climb onto the sleigh. I know exactly what he means.

Uncle Henry snaps the reins. For a long time he doesn't say much as we follow a bumpy path out of camp, but sometimes he hums a jaunty tune that is the exact opposite kind of music you should be hearing as you wade into the thick, shadowy woods. Anything could be hiding in these quiet trees: desperadoes, wolves, cold-blooded killers.

"Did you hear the wolf last night?" Uncle Henry finally speaks, keeping his eye on the path and ducking branches that threaten to pull off his cap.

I had heard that wolf, and I wasn't so sure it was simply a wolf. The dark and dangerous surroundings are making me feel a little spooked.

"How much do you know about the fellas here?" I ask, picking at a patch on my knee.

"Well," Uncle Henry says thoughtfully, "a lot of them come back every year. Some farm in the summers, log in the winters; some are running from things they're not so proud of; some have pasts they can't quite escape. . . ."

"I heard that Stinky Pete killed a man," I blurt out.

"Huh?" Uncle Henry asks. "Well, technically, yes, he did. If by 'Stinky Pete' you mean Peter McLachlan?"

"Yeah. Stinky Pete. I knew it! I never did like the cut of his jib." I shake my head.

"You do know that he used to be a preacher, not a pirate, right? And that no one calls him Stinky Pete?"

"They don't know him like I do, Uncle Henry." I squeeze my lips together and say a little prayer for his soul.

"Peter is one of the best men I've got, a true man in every sense of the word. Any discussion regarding his past is off-limits and Peter won't talk about it—he was just a boy—so do *not* bring it up. The War of Rebellion was hard on a lot of folk, men and women. My uncle Jeb returned a different man." He shakes his head. I feel like all our head shaking is going to knock our brains back to Sunday, and I'm not sure if my head is shaking in disbelief or because after an hour in this sleigh, on this rough path, everything feels shaky.

Uncle Henry looks directly at me. "And how, son, do you think you know Peter better than I do?" He shoves his cap up and scratches his head. "You just met him about six weeks ago."

"It doesn't take long to get to know a man like that. I can tell by his eyes." I point to each of mine just in case Uncle Henry doesn't know what eyes are. He appears to want to say something, but then thinks better of it.

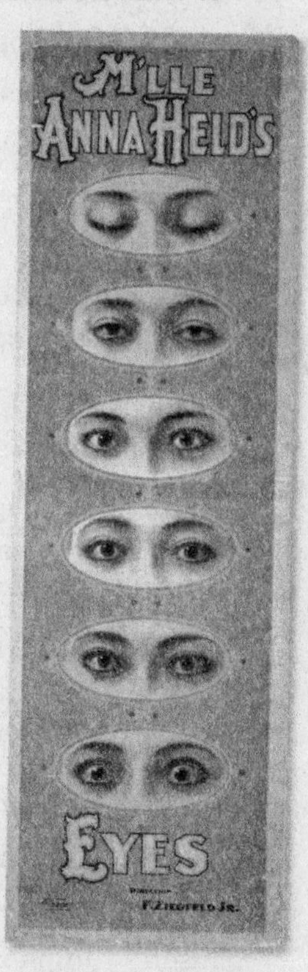

These are EYES.
Just in case
I wasn't clear.

Probably because there is no arguing with that kind of logic.

I do agree that Stinky Pete is kind of nice. For a cold-blooded killer, that is. I am proud to say I am too smart for that trap. No matter how many times that guy messes up my hair, slips me a peppermint, or shows me a new card trick, I am not going to be fooled. That's usually when the killers get you, as soon as you let down your guard.

As we get closer to where the men are working, we pass through bare spots where cutting was done earlier in the year. Trees spring up at random, lucky not to be chosen for felling, surrounded by the remains of the giants that stood around them. Branches, stumps, and pine needles sprinkle the snowy ground like dark stubble on a pale man's chin.

"Timberrrr!" shoots through the forest, the earth shakes, and the sound of a tree falling, shredding everything in its path, is like a cannon.

Uncle Henry looks me square in the eye. "Now, Stan, don't you dare wander off."

I am just about sure I have never entertained the thought of "wandering off."

"Oh, yeah? What about the time your poor mother couldn't find you in Mason's Department Store because you had gone behind the counter to pour yourself a fountain drink, eh?"

"Pffft," I assure him. "I was so little then."

"Stan," Uncle Henry says seriously, "that happened when we were at your house in October, four short months ago."

"Right. That's when I was ten. I'm practically twelve now. Big difference, there, Uncle Henry."

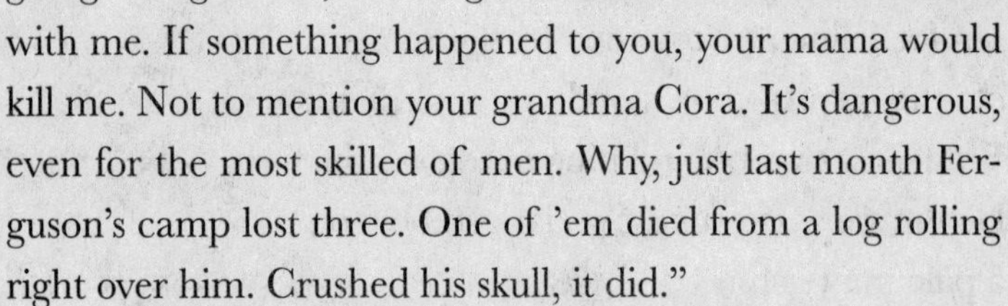

Uncle Henry gives up arguing. "Regardless, stick right with me. If something happened to you, your mama would kill me. Not to mention your grandma Cora. It's dangerous, even for the most skilled of men. Why, just last month Ferguson's camp lost three. One of 'em died from a log rolling right over him. Crushed his skull, it did."

A team of horses approaches, and the teamsters yell at Uncle Henry, "Save some chuck for us!"

"Looks good, boys!" Uncle Henry yells to them as they

clop by. "Not bad. Not a World's Fair load, but can't complain." He looks pleased.

The whole state was proud of the picture of the load of lumber headed to the 1893 Chicago World's Fair, a load so high the horses look like big dogs in front of a skyscraper. Postcards of it were sent coast to coast.

We pull into the logging operations, and Uncle Henry jumps from the sleigh to survey the scene.

Pale piles of sawdust cover most of the snowy ground. Two men stand on either side of a giant felled log, sliding a crosscut saw back and forth like wheels hitched together on a locomotive. Another guy chops the limbs off a tree lying on the ground, while above my head, dots of red are spattered throughout the trees, from high in the branches to deeper in the woods, and I stare all around me.

Blood.

"That's not blood, Stan," Uncle Henry reassures me. "That's the shanty boys' clothing—their sashes and checkered caps and socks. Easier to see them that way. And when it's easier to see them, there's less likelihood of an accident."

So much is going on around me, I can't keep it all straight. Uncle Henry bends to my level and points. "See over there? That's Danny O'Sullivan and Ole Oleson. Best sawyers in all the Upper Peninsula."

"Well, I don't think you're getting your money's worth out of them, Uncle Henry." I pat his arm sympathetically. Those guys aren't doing anything but walking around a tall tree, then walking around it again in the opposite direction. Then they look up into the sky and nod to each other.

I could do that. I am a whiz at looking up into the sky, I don't mind saying. And I'm even better at nodding.

"Just watch." Uncle Henry sits on a felled log and stares at Danny. All of a sudden, Danny walks around the tree, whips out his ax, whacks bark off the tree, and chops a V in the trunk. Then he and Ole move on to another pine.

"See that? Right there! A couple of bang-up sawyers." Uncle Henry slaps his leg with a satisfied laugh and starts building a fire.

"I don't mean to tell you how to do your job, Uncle Henry," I say modestly, although the guy obviously needs some tips, "but in case you haven't noticed, the tree is still standing. I thought the whole purpose of this operation was to cut *down* the trees."

Uncle Henry sighs. "That's just the first step, Stan. They have to figure out the best direction for the tree to fall, chop off the bark, notch it, and then when they return they'll use their crosscut saws to cut down the tree. Bam! The tree will drop exactly where they want it. It's almost magical, really." He looks all dreamy.

Sure enough, Danny and Ole return with a large two-handled saw and wordlessly start sawing into the pine, making sure the saw doesn't get pinched in the cut of the tree, sawdust shedding on the ground like blood from a wound.

"Now go get those lunches."

In a matter of minutes Uncle Henry has the fire going and coffee simmering over it. I've pulled all the food off the sled and started slapping baked beans, mashed potatoes, and roast beef onto cold tin plates. Once Uncle Henry clangs his triangle, I know the food will be gone like . . .

"Like my last paycheck?" Cager sneaks up behind me with his plate and fork. He squats next to me, ready to be the first to dig in. "Didja put a good word in for me with that mama of yours?"

I want to like that guy, but it would be a lot easier if he would keep my mama out of it.

CHAPTER 19

We get to camp as dusk turns the sky from milky blue to dull gray. I help Uncle Henry with the horses and head to the kitchen just in time for dinner prep. As I near the cook shanty, a silvery noise seems to skip over the snow like moonlight on snowflakes. It almost sounds like Mama's laughter, but I'm not sure—it's been a long time since I heard her laugh.

When I enter the kitchen, I realize that while I might have a hard time liking Cager, *this* guy is much worse. He's standing with his back to me, talking to Mama. Her hair curls around her face like a fancy frame, and her cheeks are tinged with pink. Her eyes sparkle like the lake on a bright summer day as she lets out a little giggle.

I don't like it. Not one bit.

"Oh, Stan!" She spies me. "Come meet Mr. Archibald Crutchley. He's here from town, checking on the camp for Mr. Weston."

She makes me face this intruder.

"How do you do, Mr. Slater," Mr. Crutchley says slowly like I don't understand English or would like to be called Mister. He sticks out his clean hand with a smile. His thin mustache is crisp, his bowler hat is squared perfectly on his round face, and his long coat shows just the hint of a glistening gold chain attached to his pocket watch.

I glare at him but shake his hand anyway. I've got manners, despite what Granny says.

"We were just talking about you," Mama says.

I whip my head toward her. "What exactly were you saying?" But she's already forgotten me as she picks up the conversation where they left off. She seems like she barely touches the floor as she sets the tables. Mr. Crutchley's eyes follow her.

It's inappropriate.

"So you're here for a couple of days, Mr. Crutchley?" she asks.

He nods and smiles as he takes a dainty sip of tea.

I slink away to our room only to find Granny.

"What's going on in there?" Granny is flipping through

a *Harper's Weekly.* The issue is an old one with a monkey on the cover.

I would like to own a monkey. And a tarantula.

A monkey would be a very entertaining companion out here in the woods—definitely more fun than Geri. And even a poisonous spider would be more enjoyable than Granny.

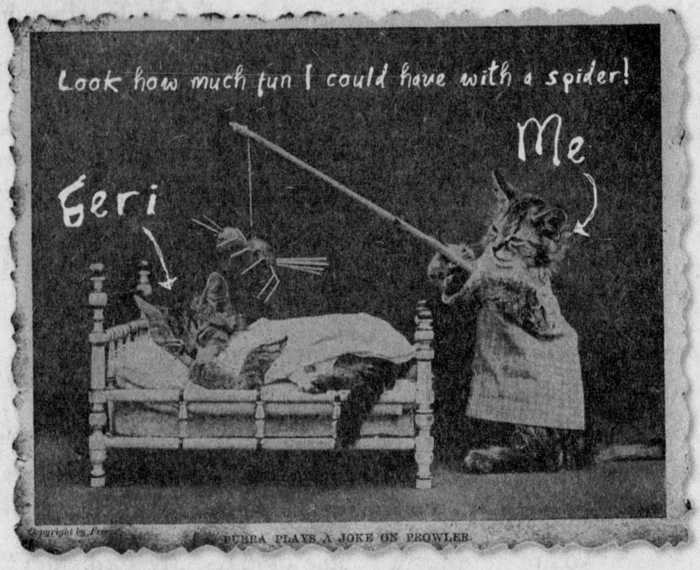

"Just Mama talking to some dumb man," I reply.

Granny looks up from her magazine. "Who?" she asks with more interest than is necessary.

I guess I should be glad it's not Stinky Pete.

"You do realize no one calls him Stinky Pete, correct?"

I close my eyes. What she doesn't know won't kill her. Unless Stinky Pete kills her; then what she doesn't know *will* kill her. It's all making my head spin. I'm bone weary from my day with Uncle Henry and want to take off my boots and grab a little snooze.

"You have about half an hour, and then we have to get dinner on the table. Go ahead and climb into your bunk, Mr. Overdramatic." Granny seems surprisingly unruffled this afternoon.

I hear laughter from the other room. It's Mr. Crutchley, and it makes me want to slug him in the jaw.

"Oh, settle down, boy," Granny snipes from behind her magazine.

I sit at the table while I loosen the ties on my boots.

"Take your socks and hang them on the rail," Granny orders without looking up.

"You know, I'm not the only one who stinks in this place," I say. "It might be nice to spray a little of that good-smelling lady stuff around from time to time." I give her a knowing look as I peel the socks from my feet. Granny wrinkles her nose and waves her hand toward the door. It's true. These socks are pretty ripe. Then again, so is Granny.

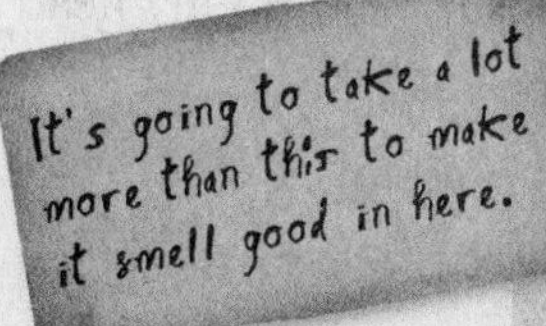

"Excuse me? Would you care to repeat yourself?" Granny drops her magazine and glares at me, her pinchy fingers at the ready.

"I said, um, 'Where's a pen? Sums are dandy!'" Which is not the finest example of thinking on my feet. And is the reason I am now doing arithmetic rather than curling up in my bunk reading *Huck Finn* in the flickering light of the kerosene lamp.

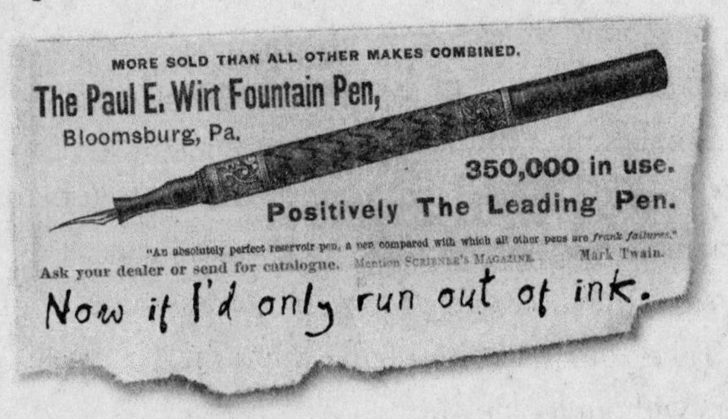

One of these days I will learn to keep my mouth shut.

"I highly doubt it," Granny says.

I pull out my copybook.

I bought candy for 10¢ and a knife for 25¢. What was the cost of both?

Honestly, this is nothing short of mental torture. I don't have two pennies to rub together. I can't buy candy or a knife, so what kind of question is this? One to bring me down into the depths of depression, that's for sure. I drop my head in my hands, and Granny flicks the top of my ear.

"Youch! You are one mean old woman!" I yelp.

“All you have to do is add ten plus twenty-five. How did you become so melodramatic? You’re worse than Geri.”

Humph. I go on to the next problem:

LESSON XXXVIII.

How many swallows can you count in the picture? How many are flying ~~inside the shed?~~ up Granny's nose? How many are at rest? How many are flying outside the shed?

1. How many birds are three times four birds?
2. How many are 3 times 4?
3. There are four nests over the door-way: if there are four eggs in each nest, how many eggs are there in all the nests? Enough for breakfast!
4. How many are 4 times 4? —I'm hungry.
5. Each swallow has two wings: how many wings have eight swallows?
6. How many are 8 times 2?

(41)

Whoever wrote this book does not know what a real problem is. A real problem has to do with bossy women, finding a father, or coming up with a quick way to prove you're a man and get to a river drive, all while wearing a flowery apron. It does not involve dealing with birds in a shed. Do you know what I'd do if I had a bunch of those birds in my shed? I'd grab a broom and whoosh them out of there, that's what. Problem solved.

Laughter from Mama and that Crutchley person shimmies in through a crack in the doorway. It's the absolute truth to describe the laughter as completely and utterly sinister. That would not be an exaggeration.

"Do you hear them, Granny? That Crutchley fellow is up to no good, I tell you. You should have seen the way he was looking at Mama," I say.

"I will remind you your mother has not been this happy in quite some time, and Mr. Crutchley is a fine, respectable gentleman. You are working yourself into a stew for nothing. The two have just met, and Mr. Crutchley returns to town in a couple days."

I release the breath I didn't realize I was holding. Granny's right. One afternoon of conversation does not mean anything. Granny has earned herself a reduced Evil Rating of 90.8 percent. Compared to Mr. Crutchley, she's an angel.

Um. Don't quote me on that.

"Although an educated gentleman such as Mr. Crutchley might be a good match for Alice, and a wonderful influence on you." Granny nods at me and then heads to the kitchen.

I can't even begin to mull over what she said. It's still possible for my real father to return, but I'll admit, time is ticking. The river drive is getting closer, and since I haven't been very good at proving my own manliness, I might need to find a substitute dad to get me where I need to go. A "somewhat" father. But I'll definitely need to be the one to choose him. Judging by Mama's recent actions, I'm starting to doubt her taste in men. And I have a hunch Granny would not be helpful in this matter, either. I think we can all agree she is not to be trusted.

No, I much prefer the father whose letters are in my Scrapbook. I may have made him up, but that doesn't mean he doesn't exist.

CHAPTER 20

Hoots slip across the icy streets of camp and into the kitchen, where I'm once again peeling potatoes. Mama is at her regular post, stirring pots at the stove and washing dishes, quietly humming some hymn. She smiles at me briefly and tweaks my nose, her eyes a bit shinier and her smile a bit more ready than just a few weeks ago.

"In the name of all that is holy"—Granny closes her eyes and pinches the bridge of her nose with her floury fingers—"can't those nincompoops next door go one Sunday without causing a major ruckus? I have had it up to here with those pathetic songs the shanty boys all sing. I just thank the good

Lord alcohol is not allowed on the premises." Granny kneads the cinnamon roll dough like it's a lumberjack's head.

Her yammering distracts me as I clean out the stove. "Goldang it!" I yelp when hot ash hits my finger. Granny grabs the top of my ear so tight, my eyes start to complain and the burn on my knuckle feels like a kiss from a kitten.

"I've had more than enough of this language, Stanley Arthur Slater." I think now is not the time to remind her I've changed my name to Rye.

"Like the bread?" Geri asks, sweeping the floors.

"No," I hiss. But it's hard to argue when your ear is in someone's viselike grip. Plus, now that I think about it, "Okay, yes, like the bread. But it's short for Zachariah."

Granny's pinch has me twisted to the side all slantindicular. I comfort myself with the thought that she's old and should be dead soon.

"Excuse me? Would you care to repeat yourself? I'm not sure I heard you." Granny's breath smells like the camphor she insists cures everything.

"Um, which part would you like repeated?" I squeak.

"Something to do with my being 'dead soon,' perhaps?"

"Oh, no, Granny." Her grip is

getting stronger, which frankly makes it hard to think. "What I actually said was, 'What do you think of the common raccoon?'" I twist up to look at Granny. She obviously thinks I'm dumber than a box full of hammers, and Geri stops sweeping to look at me. I can tell she's wondering how I'm going to get out of this one.

"The common raccoon?" Geri looks confused.

"I've been wondering about it for a long time," I respond. "Do you think a raccoon would make a good pet?" At first, I'll admit, I was trying to distract Granny from my previous comment, but now I'm starting to actually wonder about the possibility of having a raccoon as a pet.

"What will it take to get through your thick skull?" Granny mutters as she lets go of my ear, and I untwist myself to standing.

Geri leans against her broom, puzzling over my feet. "What on earth are you sporting on those clodhoppers of yours?"

I squinch my eyes at her. Like she doesn't know. "Well." I chew over whether to call her bluff, and then decide not to give her the satisfaction. "If you must know, all but one of my socks is missing, so I'm using someone else's sock until mine turn up." I glare at her. "You wouldn't happen to know anything about this, would you?"

"Why would I?" Geri scoffs. "You look ridiculous. You've got your pants tucked into one nice red sock, and the other leg is jammed into one of Granny's stockings. And why didn't you borrow one of the shanty boys' socks if you couldn't find yours? Or Daddy's?"

"Granny didn't think it was a good idea when they only have a couple pairs and need them for work. Plus, have you smelled those socks?" I wave my hand in front of my nose for emphasis. I feel a little self-conscious, because Granny's stocking is very obviously an old lady's stocking—it's long and black and thin as hosiery, and with my pants tucked in, it looks doubly ridiculous. And very unmanly.

"Do you think anyone else will notice?" I ask Geri.

"Oh, not at all." She laughs sarcastically. I give her a smirk in return and vamoose out of the cook shanty to dump the ashes and get away from these women.

As soon as I open the door, the entire mood changes. The thumping sounds coming from the bunkhouse lure me in like I'm a cat chasing a feather. I'm pulled toward the rickety shack, which seems to be jumping up and down with the sound of harmonica music, but just as I reach the door, it swings open and I'm face to face with Cager. He startles when he sees me, and he raises an eyebrow when he notices Granny's stocking. But then he winks, places a finger to his lips, and holds the door open for me.

Smells drift out so strongly they could be solid. I fight through them to slide against the wall closest to the exit with the hope that no one sees me. As much as it hurts, I have to take a breath, and as soon as I do, I realize breathing is highly overrated. This place smells like a cow died in here after eating some of Mrs. Cavanaugh's vinegar pie and kissing a wet skunk.

Once my eyes adjust to the smoky haze coming off the fire, the sizzle of Ole Oleson's chewing tobacco landing on the stove, and the unsteady shiver of the kerosene lamps hanging from the rafters, I almost forget the smell. George Frankovich sits on the seat that runs along the wall, darning his red socks while four men play cards in the corner.

One of the sawyers, Quill Mercer, whistles while he sharpens his ax on the grindstone. He nods when he sees me. Last night after dinner he told me all about his wife and little boy and the farm he hopes to get going in the spring, now that cleared land is so cheap. "I'll be home soon," he said, carving a notch in the wall outside the cook shanty. Lots of notches fill that wall.

"That's how many days we've been here," Quill told me. "Sometimes I don't know if it's better to keep count or better to forget."

"Do you want to go home?" I asked. "Do you miss them?"

Quill scratched the top of his head with the tip of his knife and then started whittling a twig. "I never wanted to leave," he said.

"Then why did you?" I asked.

"Because"—he looked up at me, the moonlight and his breath sending shivers in the air between us—"real men provide for their families." He paused. "But they always return."

I think that when I have a family, I'll never leave them. That way there's no chance I might not return.

Quill handed me a bird he whittled out of the twig and told me he once had a baby girl he always called Birdie. Then he spit on the ground, tugged on his beard, rested his hand on my head for a brief moment, and headed to the bunkhouse.

I feel the bird in my pocket as I watch flecks of light bounce off the fresh metal. Quill spins the grindstone and I'm hypnotized, watching it go round and round to the beat of Mac MacDonald's harmonica and the stomping of feet.

Stinky Pete grabs Pepper Steffel and hurls him around in a weird sort of jig. I can't help tapping my feet a little, the tune is so catchy. Larch Dougall lies in bed, covered with blankets, his toque still on his head. He's reading his Bible and murmuring to himself. Lester Finch lies next to him. He looks like he's trying to sleep, but good luck with that. I say a little prayer of thanks, since it's Sunday and all, that I don't have to share my bunk with anyone, let alone Lester Finch. He is known to be a little gassy. Plus, I'm pretty sure he is fake sleeping.

"Ain't that the truth!" Stinky Pete hollers over the din. "Not nobody going to sleep with this racket going on!" Then he grabs my elbow and swings me, and suddenly I'm in the middle of a circle of tangy-smelling men, all of them hooting and hollering to beat the band.

This is more fun than a barrel full of monkeys.

I am a whiz at the dancing, I don't mind saying, but I'm pretty much dead when Slim Heil starts tuning his fiddle, so I plop on the nearest bunk to listen. Someone drags Truman Sharpe to his feet and makes him sing the "Lumberjack's Alphabet," which is so much better than the alphabet I learned in school.

A is for ax, which we swing to and fro.
B is for boys that handle them so.
C is for cant hooks, the logs we make spin.
D is for danger that we're always in.

Then Slim slows the tempo right down. All the shanty boys start singing, quiet at first, a sad song about death and river drives.

They had not rolled off many logs when
the boss to them did say,
"I'd have you be on your guard, brave boys.
That jam will soon give way."
But scarce the warning had he spoke when
the jam did break and go,
And it carried away these six brave youths
and their foreman, young Monroe.

When the rest of the shanty boys these
sad tidings came to hear,

To search for their dead comrades to
the river they did steer.
One of these a headless body found,
to their sad grief and woe,
Lay cut and mangled on the beach the
head of young Monroe.

I might have drifted off for a moment, thinking about the river drive and poor Monroe's head. The river drive must be on everyone's mind now that the sun is up earlier in the morning and the roof occasionally lands a drip of melted snow on your tongue or, if your aim is bad, smack-dab in your eye. And even though the song is sad, I can tell the shanty boys who will be staying for the river drive are champing at the bit to prove their skills and take charge of the river.

I have a hazy dream of being on top of a twirling, birling log in the middle of the water, twisting and jumping, and Lydia Mae with her bouncy curls cheering from the shore. But I soon realize it's actually a nightmare. Granny stands in front of me, one hand on her hip, the other sticking a finger in Stinky Pete's face, and the twirling I feel is Granny pulling me off the bunk. Her words glide through my foggy head until I can make sense of them. The room was so noisy before, but now it's like the funeral parlor after Great-Aunt Sophie died. Except quieter.

Granny grabs me by the ear and marches me through the door like I'm a horse being led to the glue factory. I glance back at fifty sorry-looking lumberjacks appearing as ashamed as I felt when I "borrowed" Mrs. Cavanaugh's pink underdrawers from the clothesline last summer and gave them to Conrad McAllister to wear on his head.

"What on earth were you thinking?" Granny jerks me out of my daydream. "There's not enough hot water in the world to clean the cooties off you now. Are you aware what filth lies in that den of iniquity? I wouldn't be surprised if your very soul needs the blessing of three priests and a Baptist preacher." Her blathering goes on until I find myself in a vat of hot water up to my neck, covering my privates with a towel.

"Hold still!" Geri commands as she works kerosene all over my scalp "just in case." Granny is boiling my clothes on the stove. Also just in case.

I would like my mama. Just in case.

"She has dinner to take care of and much on her mind," Granny says.

Geri yaps on about the history of lice. How

they might cause diseases. "It's possible you now have typhus. I would keep an eye out for a rash and fever, maybe a cough."

"Oh, come on!" I can't help exclaiming. I am certainly not falling for this a third time.

Geri stops scrubbing. "Seriously, Stan. That bunkhouse is a breeding ground for germs. I'm not kidding."

I look at Granny to save me, but she just shakes her head and shrugs, and Geri starts in on my scalp again.

Suddenly I feel itchy.

"It's not entirely impossible you won't up and die."

Geri is so much fun.

I don't think I'll be spending any more time in the bunkhouse, but it sure was nice while it lasted.

My head spins, and not from the smell of the kerosene. When we passed through the kitchen, I noticed crotchety Mr. Crutchley talking to Mama. Why is that man still here making Mama look as if she's spent the afternoon at a picnic, causing her to laugh like a schoolgirl, and leaving me alone with Granny and Geri?

Now Geri's talking cooties again. I hope against hope none show up in my bed, since Granny left the bedbug poison back in town, and I don't want her to clean our bunk with salt pork grease like she did when we first got here.

I do love bacon. I just don't want to sleep in it.

I dunk my head and stay underwater because it's the only place that's quiet.

Geri pulls me up by my hair and inspects me while I

work at keeping all my unmentionable parts covered. "I'm pretty sure you have effluvia."

I know my little trip to the bunkhouse has cheated death, so I catch my breath, tilt my head, and look her straight in the eyes. "What is that? And how long do I have to live?"

Geri forces my head down toward the water so she can scrub the back of my neck.

"I honestly don't know. I just like saying that word. Effluvia. Effluvia."

She has a point.

Effluvia.

Dear Son,

I have been stuck in a sanitarium and have been unable to write. Effluvia is no joke. Neither is yellow fever, spontaneous combustion, or quinsy. I've had them all and lived to tell the tale. Unfortunately, I have been treated by a lady doctor! Can you imagine such a thing? She's very bossy and ugly and smells like feet. Plus, she has no idea what she's talking about.

When I get out of here, I will send you a medical bag filled with sharp things like needles, syringes, and knives. Please don't tell Geri. She would want her own medical bag, and she'd have no idea what to do with it.

I'm also sending you your very own rolling chair because you really shouldn't have to walk around so much.

From,
Dad

CHAPTER 21

After a couple months in a logging camp, things fall into a routine. I get up before the sun and chop some firewood with my baby-sized hatchet, fire up the stove, and help with serving breakfast to all the shanty boys. Then I eat all the rest of the bacon, some flapjacks, and a doughnut before Granny scolds me for being a bottomless pit. Then I try to hide where Granny can't find me.

Right now Geri and I are in the van with Uncle Henry, playing dominoes away from Granny and her evil mathematical ways.

I'm winning. Maybe not technically, but I have a strategy. I am a whiz at the games, I don't mind saying.

"Chickie five."

"What? Again?" Of course I have no fives. "Pass."

And that's when I see Mr. Archibald Crutchley coming in, carrying a crate in front of him like he doesn't want to get his overcoat dirty. He's been at camp so often in the last few weeks, it's like he works here.

"He does work here, Stan," Geri remarks. "He works for Mr. Weston overseeing all of his camps. How can you not know this?"

"Here's the tobacco you needed, Henry. And something else—maybe it's medicine?" Mr. Crutchley hands the crate to Uncle Henry, dusts imaginary dirt from his coat, and smooths his mustache.

"Yep. The boys have been going through both. Don't get paid if they miss any work."

Mr. Crutchley shakes his fancy city coat and sweeps his hat from his head like he's going to stay awhile.

"Well, hello, kids." He smiles at us and pops a peppermint into his mouth, offering one to each of us.

"Don't mind if I do," Uncle Henry says.

"Thank you, Mr. Crutchley," Geri says sweetly, drawing a smile from the man. Obviously he's easily fooled.

"Stan?"

I grab one but glare at him and don't say thanks.

"What is your problem?" Geri hisses at me.

"I know things, missy," I hiss back at her.

Uncle Henry and Mr. Crutchley lean over the ledger, nodding and scratching their heads and pointing at the little scribbles marking the pages. Their backs are to us and they may have forgotten we're even here.

"Chickie threes," Geri says. "I win." Winner always has to put the game away, which sometimes makes it better to lose.

"It's never better to lose," Geri reminds me.

Before I can come up with a smart response, I hear my mama's name being tossed around like a hoop with a stick.

ON THE HEATH.—From a drawing by Robert W. Macbeth.

"So, you think Alice is ready?" Mr. Crutchley stares intently at Uncle Henry.

"Well, when they first arrived a couple months ago, I would have said no, but now I think there's a good possibility she might be open to the idea."

"So you think there's a chance?" Mr. Crutchley's cheeks are pink, which isn't very manly.

I lean toward them, straining to hear what they're saying.

"Well, it's nice if Alice is sweet on you, but Cora's the one you have to worry about. If she likes you, you're set. If she doesn't, well, you're out of luck. She chose Alice's first husband." Uncle Henry nods thoughtfully.

"Wasn't he a no-good skunk?" Mr. Crutchley purses his lips.

I am just about to defend my poor, defenseless father when Geri whispers in my ear. "Granny is *not* choosing my husband," she says, her hair a tangle of cinnamon curls and her apron covered in spots of blood, which would scare me if I didn't know her history of mutilating raw chickens.

I pity any man Geri calls her husband.

"Well, to be perfectly fair, the guy was a charmer. He had Cora completely fooled, and she's been trying to fix that mistake ever since. That's why she's doubly interested in Alice's next husband—it's a chance for her to save face."

If I were Granny, I would *not* save that face. I would definitely get a new one.

"I would be a very beneficial match for young Alice," Mr. Crutchley says, twirling the end of his mustache.

"You know she's divorced, right?" Uncle Henry says quietly. "Arthur stopped sending any money and sent her divorce papers back in late December, so it's all pretty recent."

I slap my hand over my mouth. That was what was in the envelope? Divorce papers? My sweet Mama is divorced?

Geri pretends to be busy putting the dominoes away, and I drop my eyes as if I'm helping her. The minute a grown-up knows you're listening, they start talking about things like the weather or their great-aunt's gout.

Mr. Crutchley gives a serious nod. "I know divorce tarnishes a lady, but I might just be willing to overlook this for a woman as fine as Alice. Is she still hung up on her ex-husband?" He's fishing for information, even though he looks like he's more interested in his fingernail.

"That husband of hers was a no-good lout. Land sakes, it's common knowledge divorce is a black mark on a woman's name, but we never saw hide nor hair of the cussed fool in the last eleven years." I have rarely heard Uncle Henry curse, so I know he is a bit worked up, and this is the most information I've ever gathered on my father. I strain to hear as Uncle Henry's voice lowers.

"He did manage to send money from time to time, I will give him that." Uncle Henry picks his teeth. "Alice finally told him he could use any excuse he wanted as long as he granted her a divorce, so Arthur claimed she deserted him."

Divorced? Deserted? I didn't know anything about a divorce, and I certainly don't want anyone to think my sweet mama is a deserter! I bolt for the door. Right now I feel like my brain is mushy water swimming between my ears, and the air around me is so thick I have to push my way through it. As soon as I get outside, I bend over gasping like I can't catch my breath. I have a father who's lost and a mother who is a deserter. What does that make me? Lost in the desert?

"You okay? Is it your asthma?" Geri asks, her face next to mine.

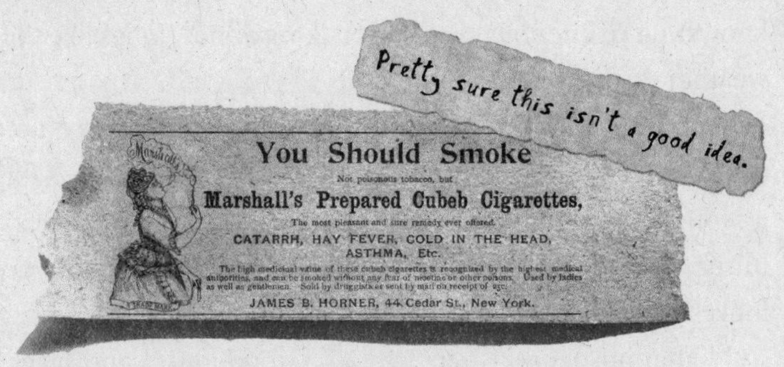

I'm afraid to say anything in case she diagnoses me with immediate death.

"Are you okay?" she repeats.

I try to catch my breath. Maybe I do have asthma. "As okay as anyone can be who has had to endure the pain and suffering I've been subjected to! I just found out Mama is divorced! And I had to listen to other people call her a deserter!" I wail.

Geri rolls her eyes and stands up. "Oh, for goodness' sake, when is the last time you even saw that so-called father of yours?"

Never. I shake my head and take the bacon Geri shoves in my face, like bacon can solve anything.

I take a bite. Bacon can solve pretty much anything.

"This is 1895!" Geri says. "Sure, women have a ways to go to ensure their equal rights, but your mama's divorce certainly does not stop her from being an important member of society. Or, for that matter, a darn good mother."

Geri shakes her finger in my face. Part of me wants to bite it. The other part of me knows she's right.

"Of course I'm right."

"But she deserted him!" I wail. I breathe deeply and stand up to look at Geri. Her eyes are slits, and she looks at me like I'm plumb crazy. "What *is* a deserter?"

"I'm glad you asked," she replies. "Technically, it's someone who abandons his responsibilities. Like a soldier in the War of Rebellion who up and leaves the army for no good reason. Often those deserters got shot."

"My mama is going to get shot?" I nearly fall over from shock.

Geri looks at me and shakes her head. "You are such a fool."

"But you just said . . ."

She closes her eyes and waves her hand like she's brushing away mosquitoes. "You have such selective hearing. Your mother is not a deserter in the War of Rebellion. In fact, she's not a deserter at all. She just told your dad to write whatever he wanted on the divorce papers so that she and *you* could get on with your lives."

I look at her skeptically. "How do you know?"

Her shoulders drop and her head tilts at me. "Are you serious? This is all news to you? My mother has been talking about what a useless, lazy bum your dad is since I was knee high. And no one else seems to have much of a problem with your mother's situation. There are at least three men vying for Aunt Alice's hand right now. I thought you knew all this—honestly, it's so obvious."

"What are you talking about?" I ask through a mouthful of bacon.

"Well . . ." She sticks up her finger and starts ticking them off. "First there's Peter. . . ."

"You mean Stinky Pete? He's a murderer! He killed a man!" Plus, he's been spending what little free time he's had with me; he hasn't had any time to court Mama.

"In the War of Rebellion, you chucklehead. According to Daddy, Peter's father was off fighting, a wayward rebel showed up, and it was either kill or have his family farm burned to the ground and his mother and sisters taken prisoner. And you are aware no one but you calls him Stinky Pete, right?" She hands me another piece of bacon. "Why do you do that, anyway?"

"Have you ever smelled him?" I ask. I must admit, it's a relief to hear Stinky Pete probably won't be murdering anyone in their sleep, but I'm still watching out for that guy. You never know, he might have an evil side.

Plus, it's more fun this way.

"They all smell the same," Geri replies.

"Well, I just think we need to keep an eye on him," I say. "Call it a hunch." I point bacon at her for emphasis and then cram it in my mouth.

"Then there's Cager." She gets a swoony look on her face and says his name the way I say "apple pie."

"What about Cager?"

"Well, he's certainly making an effort to get to know your mama." Geri looks at me like she knows something I don't.

Which, apparently, she does.

"What kind of poppycock are you spouting now?" I mumble. "When have they even had time to spend together?"

"How about when you were in the bunkhouse? How about Sundays when you're off learning card tricks or playing cribbage with Mr. McLachlan? How about evenings when you're huddled under your blankets reading whatever it is you're reading?"

I gasp. "Mama has been spending all that time with Cager?" I am truly shocked, although that might explain why she hasn't been around much.

"Well, to be fair, it's not only Aunt Alice and Cager. My ma and Granny are usually there, but he's always around. And he's just so fine-looking." She gets a faraway look in her eyes.

I am puzzled. "How can you tell he's 'fine-looking'? They all have those beards and bushy eyebrows. They all look alike."

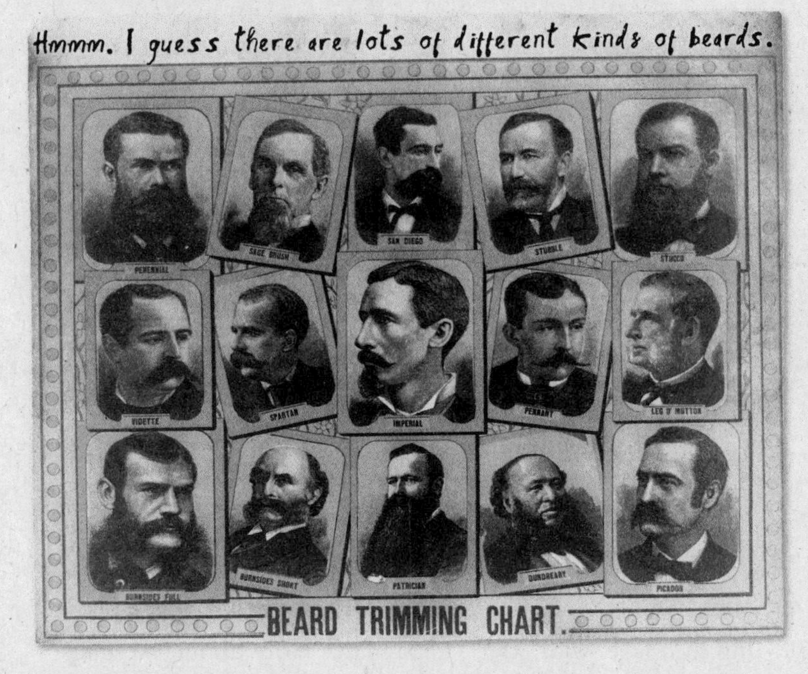

Geri ignores me as she sticks up a third finger. "Finally, Mr. Crutchley. There's a man who can provide the finer things in life for both you and your mama: bikes, books, proper medical care." She pauses to think. "And he just might be the best man to convince Granny you're ready for a little trip to the river drive. Although," she adds, "it's quite doubtful you're actually up for that adventure."

Is this what it has come to? Mr. Crutchley as a stepfather? Is the river drive worth that much? Worth losing my mama to a man who waxes his mustache, squeals when he steps in horse manure, and wipes his mouth with a hankie instead of his sleeve?

But then again, just last night Pepper Steffel told me he has a bet with Mac MacDonald that he can stay on a log in the middle of the river longer, and that's something I would sure like to see. I also imagine challenging Geri to a similar contest. And winning, of course.

But I don't want Mr. Crutchley around permanently. Maybe, just maybe, I really don't need a father, but what I do need is a man—a man who knows his way around Granny, a man who doesn't act like a namby-pamby even if he has to wear a flowery apron, a man who can almost burp the entire alphabet, or at least will be able to if he can escape his granny long enough to get some practice in.

After being at this lumber camp for a few months now, I think I know just the man.

Me.

CHAPTER 22

It should come as no surprise to anyone that manly men do manly things like crush cans with their bare hands.

"Stan, what are you doing with that can of corned beef?" Geri asks.

"Just, uh, crushing it with my bare hands," I grunt, bending over and gripping the can.

"Why don't you wait until after we actually eat the beef?"

I hesitate. That might not be such a bad idea. "Well, if you insist," I say, standing upright. Women. I will never understand them.

"Let's finish up here and then go see if we can help in the barn. They might let us feed the horses," Geri suggests. Anything to avoid Granny. I set the corned beef on the counter to deal with later and follow Geri outside.

"So," she says, "did you happen to hear Knut Knutson's cough at dinner last night?" Her hands are shoved in her pockets even though the day is warm for March, and she leans forward in thought. The only thing I heard last night was the sound of belching shanty boys, followed by Granny's snores, which would rival any sawmill.

It goes without saying I am a wee bit tired and I stifle a yawn, but Geri keeps right on talking.

"I am concerned," she continues. "It could be pleurisy, I suppose. Or perhaps typhus? You were near him, Stan. Did you notice any red spots on his body? Was it a dry cough, would you say?"

I remember Knut coughing, but I am pretty sure it was because of the piece of ham caught in his throat. He was fine after Angus Murphy slapped him on the back a few times, but I am not telling this to Geri and spoiling all her fun. Plus, if she's busy diagnosing the shanty boys, then she's not diagnosing me.

We pass Cooter the blacksmith, who's in his open doorway, flailing his arm up and down, hammering on a hot piece of metal. Pings sail out of the shop like sparks from a fire.

And then I see it. I hope Geri does not see it, but the glint of the sun off the metal is like a lighthouse beckoning a crew of seasick sailors. It's shining so brightly, I'm pretty sure it just woke up fifteen hibernating bears and a couple of woodchucks.

In other words, it's hard to miss.

A brand-spanking-new ax, fresh from Cooter's anvil and awaiting its owner.

It's sharp. It's shiny. And it scares me to high Heaven.

"Oh, Stan?" Geri stops dead in her tracks. "Do you see that?" She flips her head in the direction of the ax.

"What?" I play dumb just in case she is referring to something else, like a bunny. Or an unusual snowflake. I look around, trying to find something, anything, to divert her attention because I know what's coming next.

Geri makes a beeline for the ax. Of course. She grabs the handle and tilts it in my direction. "Hmmm. Probably too heavy for you. Probably no way you could pick up this ax and cut a piece of wood the size of a matchstick off this stump right here." She throws her leg up on the stump all Annie Oakley style, her black stockings sliding down her leg and her ankle boots a mess of mud.

Her eyes have the same glint as the sun shining off the ax, and I'm 87.6 percent sure she and the ax are equally dangerous.

“Pfft.” I exhale. “Me using an ax is the same as you playing with your paper dolls.”

Geri looks indignant and her foot slips, causing her to momentarily lose her balance. “What, Stanley Slater, are you talking about? I’m a professional! I do *not* play with paper dolls.”

“That’s not what I’ve heard,” I reply. Actually, that’s *not* what I’ve heard. I’ve never heard of her playing with paper dolls or anything else a normal kid would play with, and that’s God’s honest truth. She is weirdly grown up. But my attempt to throw Geri off track appears to be working. Or at least I’m throwing her off balance. Literally.

“I think you’re just afraid you can’t do it,” she answers, quickly regaining her balance.

“Fine.” I make my way toward the ax, walking slowly while praying someone is nearby to stop me.

Cooter’s banging is so loud, he’s practically deaf, so he’s of no use. Where is Granny when you need her?

Geri starts to let go of the ax handle, her face smug. I muster all my strength and reach to grab it before it hits the ground.

CHAPTER 23

Granny's gnarly hand appears in the corner of my eye and a smell attacks my nose. It is so foul I have obviously returned from the dead simply to deal with it.

"Well, the smelling salts seem to be doing the trick." Granny's voice seems far-off.

"Is he awake?" Mama leans over me, and her voice slides through my head like a half-tied ribbon as the dining hall comes into hazy focus.

"Stand back," a stern male voice commands. Cooter peers into my face. In his grubby left hand is a needle trailing a long thread. His blackened fingers slowly make their way to my eye.

"Arrrgh!" I yell, thrashing my arms. A shooting pain

lights up my skull. Without thinking, I reach up to my forehead, and when I pull my hand away, it's covered in blood.

"Arrrgh! I've been shot! I've been shot!"

Mama reaches across me, stopping my arms from flapping all over the place.

"You have not been shot, Stanley," she says firmly, holding my head between her hands. "You've had an accident." This time her voice is quieter, and her eyes are as reassuring as rain in June. But when I try to nod at her, the pain shoots through my brain like a bullet from a revolver, so I squeeze my eyes shut. When I open them again, I see my hands, tinted red.

"My head has been chopped off!" I'm in shock, I'm dying, and my arms go every which way. Out of the corner of my eye I see Granny, who throws her hands up in the air and rolls her eyes to the ceiling.

"Good Lord, Alice. I say let him die."

Mama leans over me again with a gentle hand on my arm. "Honey, you just had a little accident with an ax. Cooter is going to stitch it up quickly before you even know what has happened." Cooter peers over Mama's shoulder with a smile. Half of his teeth are missing, and the grime from the blacksmith shop speckles his face like a spotted egg.

"Yup." He nods. "Ready? This will only hurt for a split second." He turns his head to spit on the floor and uses his pinkie to pick something black out of his teeth.

I pinch my lips together. There is no way Cooter, with his grimy hands and toothless grin, is going to touch me. I shake my head.

"Nope," I say through gritted teeth.

"This is not an option, Stan," Mama warns.

"I won't let him do it." I look at Mama, my eyes a teensy bit damp.

"Well, you must. You need to have the cut stitched up in order for the bleeding to stop." She looks at me pleadingly as I shake my head.

"Then let Geri do it," I say.

Mama pulls back in shock. "What?" she asks.

"I said, let Geri do it. Let her stitch me up."

"Well . . ." Mama hesitates.

Granny starts to protest loudly. "No. No, no, no! Geri is a child, not a doctor. . . ."

"Neither is Cooter, and Geri is very practical," Mama says slowly.

"No! I forbid it."

Mama turns to Geri. "Do you think you could do this, Geri? Do you think you could stitch Stan's head up?"

Geri nods so hard I think her head is going to pop off her neck. "Oh, yes, ma'am! I have been waiting for this day my whole, entire life."

Mama looks me in the face. "This is what you want?"

I nod. "I won't even make a fuss. She is very good at sewing up chickens."

"Okay, then," Mama agrees.

Granny stomps off in a huff, and Geri washes her hands. Just like I knew she would.

And that's how I became Geri's first, and best, patient. Sure, the stitches are a little uneven and my head still hurts, but even Granny nodded her approval when Geri was done. Either that, or my head was all wobbly.

CHAPTER 24

"What, in the name of all that is holy, is on your face?" Granny stops kneading bread to look at me disbelievingly. She should be a little more polite. After all, I almost died just yesterday.

"Well, woman, this right here"—I stroke my chin—"is what we *men* call whiskers or facial hair."

She studies my manly stubble. "Hmmm . . . looks like someone dipped a pen in the inkwell and drew on your face."

"Humph. Shows how much you know, woman. Now where is my chow?" I do my best impression of a man. I even clear my throat and spit on the floor.

Granny hands me a towel. I take it and clean up the spit.

"Dad-blame it, but this is women's work right here. Yes siree, Bob." It's possible I'm overdoing it, but being a man is not as easy as it looks.

"Thank you," she says in clipped tones as I hand her the towel. "And your 'chow' is with everyone else's. In the oven, ready to be eaten after the lumberjacks finish their dinner. Now set the table."

"Woman, I'll set the table when I'm goldang ready," I reply in my manliest voice.

Granny's eyes sizzle, but it's Mama who grabs my collar and swings me around. "That's enough. You do not use such language or speak to your grandmother that way. When she asks you to do something, you do it. No questions asked. Do you understand me?"

I nod, and she lets go of my collar and gently moves my hair to examine my stitches. "Hmmm," she says, and hurries to stir the baked beans like nothing has happened.

I have decided; I'm ready to set the table now.

"What are you doing out of bed?" Geri asks. She's peeling potatoes over the sink. "You're supposed to be recovering."

"I'm a quick healer," I reply proudly.

I am a whiz at being a patient, I don't mind saying.

"What are you talking about? You're an awful patient! Three grown men had to lie across your body, and one had

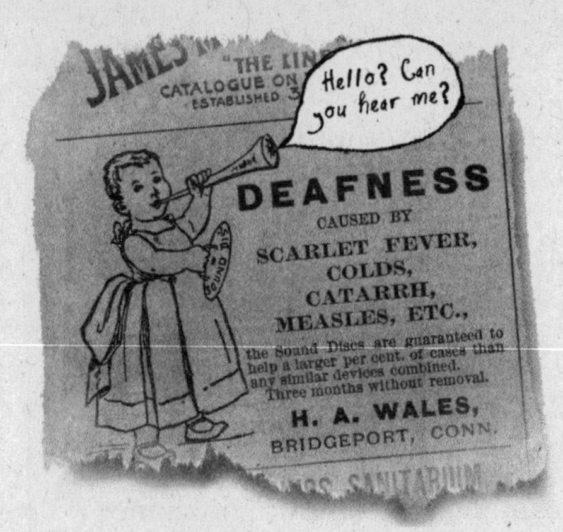

to hold your head steady. Plus, the screaming made us all pretty near deaf." Geri stares at me.

I wince because, honestly, she is loud, my head still hurts, and I might feel slightly dizzy. "Well, you can't deny I'm your *first* patient. Also, real men don't need much time to heal. Especially men who have been hit in the head with an ax." I nod knowingly. "That kind of near-death experience will change your life. And it will make you a man." I hope Mama is listening.

Geri stops peeling potatoes and stares at me. "You realize you didn't get hit in the head with the blade of an ax, don't you? You tried to pick up the ax off the ground, stumbled, and fell, cutting your head open on the wooden handle."

"You tell the story your way, I'll tell it mine," I say, and stomp to my bunk to lie down. It's been a trying afternoon.

After dinner, Mama applies kerosene to my face. She's smiling as she tries to scrub the ink off.

"Please tell me that you know drawing whiskers on your face does not make you a man," she says.

I nod. Obviously I was just trying to encourage some manly beard growth.

"And that real men don't spit or swear? That's not what makes a man a man."

She kisses my forehead, lifts my chin, and examines my

face. "Well, that will just have to do. Now stop torturing your granny, and stay away from any matches. Your face may be flammable. Better yet, go and wash." She tweaks my nose.

Even when I try my hardest, I fail at being a man. The visit to the bunkhouse didn't help. The trick with the ax simply gave me a headache and some pretty exciting stitches. And the whiskers left me with a face that could burst into flames at any minute.

This is the furthest I've ever felt from being a man. All I really want to do is cuddle up in bed and have Mama read me a book. Or play with the toy soldiers still lined up on my windowsill in the apartment house. But I can't. Because that's not manly, and being manly is the only way I'll ever understand my father, maybe know why he left and never returned, have a chance to go on the river drive, and keep Mama away from unwanted suitors.

I wonder if I'll ever be enough: old enough, manly enough, worth enough.

"Why don't we cuddle up in my bed and read *Huck Finn*?" Mama asks, like she's reading my mind. I nod my head up and down so hard, water flies from my eyes. I have all sorts of bubbly nerves popping around in my chest, and I feel like they might explode through my ears. I lean against Mama and feel her lean into me, like we're the last two pieces of a puzzle.

"Mama, why can't we go on the river drive?" I hurry to finish my thought before she shoots me down. The warmer weather and the melting snow remind me daily that I don't have much time to convince her and Granny that we should stay longer. "I would be a lot of help in the wanigan, and I could keep Geri out of trouble, and we could make some more money to get through the summer, and . . . it might be fun."

"Well, all those things are true," Mama says, resting her head on top of mine. "You are a lot of help, and we would make more money, but you left out the dangerous parts—the mass of logs that usually hurt at least one boy, if not kill him outright. And after your accident, I would be holding my breath the whole time we were there. To be perfectly honest"—she sweeps the hair off my face—"I'm tired of holding my breath."

I take a deep breath of my own. Mama's voice is like a swimming hole on a hot summer day—I know if I jump in, I'll feel better. "Why did you desert my father?" I study my knuckles as if I've never seen knuckles before.

Actually, I don't think I really *have* looked at my knuckles before.

I watch my bendy fingers wrinkle and unwrinkle and feel Mama's body stiffen. She sighs, and then lifts my chin and makes me meet her eyes. Even after hours working in the kitchen, even after getting little sleep in the bunk she shares with Sawmill Granny, even after having to deal with my near death from a fatal blow of an ax—even after all that, her skin looks like cream just poured from the bottle, and her eyes are clear and shiny.

"Honey, I don't know where you got your information. . . ."

"Unc—"

She puts two fingers to my lips. "You know I didn't really desert your father. At least it's not quite like that." She looks down like maybe there's a spot of dirt on the floor, and when she looks back up, her eyes are all floaty. "I am so, so sorry."

"Why?" I ask. "Sorry about what?" I'm worried that she's going to tell me something bad, something like I'm going to be Granny's kitchen slave. Or she's marrying Mr. Crutchley.

I don't know which is worse.

"Just, well, that I don't have a father for you." She lowers her head, and her shoulders shake. "I never imagined . . . I always wanted . . . It's not what . . ."

I pat her like she might break, then do the only thing I can think of.

I hand her a hankie.

"Can you tell me anything about him?" I ask.

Mama gently blows her nose. "Well, he was handsome."

"Of course." I nod, and Mama smiles and messes up my hair. "But what is he *like*? Does he read? Is he rich? Does he hunt rhinos in Africa? Did he explore the North Pole?" I'm on the edge of my seat.

"Honestly, he might do all those things, honey," Mama replies. I nod furiously because, well, I knew it! "Or none of them," she continues, but I choose to ignore that part. "He was funny and impulsive"—she looks at me knowingly—"and loved to travel, which made his job on the railroad so perfect for him. He was not one to be tied down."

I nod. I completely understand not wanting to be tied down.

"And where is he?" I stare at her intently, but Mama just squeezes her lips together and shakes her head.

"I don't know. I wish I could tell you, but I just don't know." She shrugs. "And honestly, maybe I don't wish I could tell you. There's a big part of me that's afraid he'll hurt you, not know how great you are, not see in you all the traits that will make you a wonderful man and father someday."

I can't bring myself to ask her how I'm supposed to know what a good man or father is like when no one has ever been around to show me.

"Maybe you can look at all the men in your life who are solid examples of good men who appreciate you, and worry less about the one man who doesn't. Or just imagine your father as the best kind of man there is," Mama continues as if she's reading my mind again. Which is a little worrisome, to tell the truth. There's a lot of stuff in there no one should know. "But don't expect him to return, Stan. Just don't set yourself up for that. I know how that feels. You are a good, good son. You always ask me if I need help peeling potatoes or setting the table, you make sure I have my coat when I run outside, and you make me laugh like no one else in the world." My heart feels warm the more she talks. "And trust me when I say that if being a good son means you'll be a good father, you have nothing to worry about."

I must say, I feel a little relieved to know I probably won't grow up to become a rapscallion, scalawag, or hooligan (unless I want to, of course). But this entire conversation has me feeling a bit like I have mud between my ears. I thought the more I knew about my father, the closer I would be to finding him. But I don't even know him as well as I know Stinky

Pete. And I have no better idea about what makes a man manly than I did before I came here.

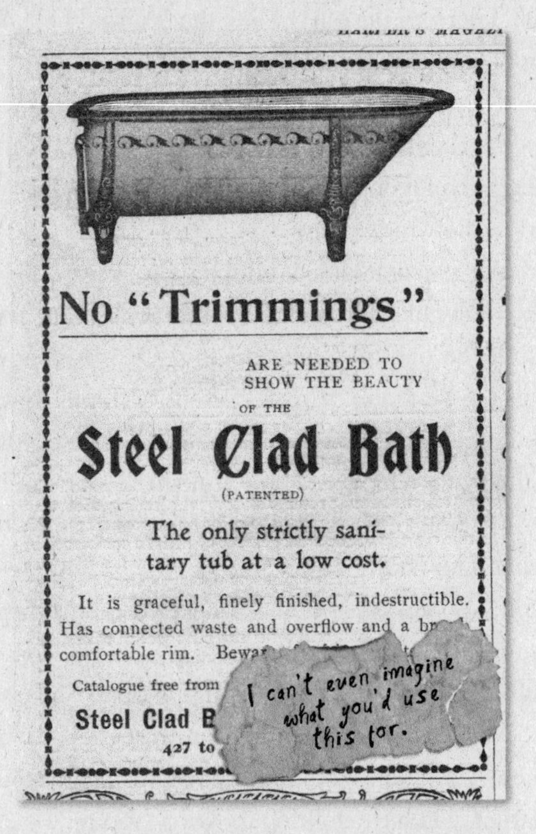

Sometimes it seems fun: you get to swear and spit and smell like bathtubs were never invented. Other times it seems like being a man is bigger than that, like when Stinky Pete swept the floor after I dropped a plate, before Granny even caught me. Or when Uncle Henry told Mr. Crutchley it was his fault Ole Oleson got hurt out on the site. I happen to know from overhearing all the guys at dinner that Ole had told Cager that he "grew on people—just like a wart." Cager slugged him a good one, and Ole was out for two days. If Mr. Crutchley had known about the fight, Ole and Cager might have been out for good.

I'm not sure I'm ready for the not-fun part of being a grown-up.

I did write down that wart joke, however. I need some new material for insulting Conrad McAllister.

Mama squeezes me next to her. "My little man," she says, smiling. Which is true. Except for the little part.

"Now can we go to the river drive?" I ask. I'm very hopeful this time will be a big, fat yes.

She looks me right in the eye and grins. "No. No, no, a thousand times no. You dodged a bullet with that last accident, Stan. I am not pushing our luck."

I'm speechless. Which doesn't happen often.

"Plus, I have plans for us. Big plans that will change our lives. Now go get ready and hop into bed or we won't have any time to read."

I'm afraid to ask what the big plans are. I'm pretty sure they will not involve a wanigan but a man, and I don't mean a "somewhat" man like me.

CHAPTER 25

When I snuggle up to Mama and hear all about Huck Finn's adventures on the mighty Mississippi, it sounds so much like how I imagine the river drive would be, it's more than I can take. So I pretend to fall asleep.

Fake sleeping is a tried-and-true way to learn all sorts of things—things adults would never say in front of you if you were awake. I keep my eyes closed except I can see a little bit through the fringe of my eyelashes.

"Here you go, honey. It should help." Granny pulls money from her apron pocket and secures it in Mama's hand. She is buying me for her work slave, I just know it. Or to trade for pickles.

"What is this?" Mama holds the money like it's a poisonous snake.

"It's for you. I've been saving it," Granny says in her no-nonsense voice.

"For what?" Mama keeps staring at the money like she doesn't know what to do with it.

"I know your plans, and I fully approve. Stanley's accident simply confirmed the fact that it's time for you to leave. It's my small way of helping, and I'll hear no ifs, ands, or buts about it," Granny says.

"So you think it's the right thing to do?" Mama asks.

My eyes pop open. Of course it's not the right thing to do! I don't deserve to spend the rest of my life as that woman's slave! And I'm worth a whole lot more than pickles.

Granny puts her arm around Mama's shoulder like she hasn't heard me say a thing. Because, guess what? She hasn't heard me say a thing! I'm getting good at this thinking-in-your-head business. "Of course it's right. Stan will be just fine in St. Ignace." Granny gives Mama a squeeze. "A fresh start for both of you, without anything stopping you or anyone talking behind your back, is a good thing. It's time to stop waiting and make your own destiny. And it's hard to pass up such an opportunity."

St. Ignace? Where in the heck is St. Ignace? And who thinks we need a fresh start? I'm perfectly content with my life and friends in Manistique. Especially Lydia Mae and her dark, curly hair. I'm not so sure I'd miss Conrad.

But I'm frozen to the mattress, even though the straw is poking me in the cheek.

"And when you and Archibald get married . . ."

I'm like a corpse awakened from the dead. My eyes pop open and I'm about to yell when Mama says something I never thought I would hear her say.

"No, Mother, I am not going to marry Mr. Crutchley."

I can tell Granny is taken aback. Her head jerks and she looks at Mama like lightning has struck her and set her hair on fire.

"What did you say?" Granny's tone is sharp, her eyes are slits, and her breath looks like icicles could form on her very words.

But I have to hand it to Mama. She draws herself up, taller than Granny by a head, and repeats: "No, Mother."

Granny's mouth drops. "What do you mean, 'no'? I thought you were enjoying his company. Archibald Crutchley is a fine man who will provide for you and Stanley. It is apparent both of you need a man around. You cannot handle that boy on your own, and I don't know what you would have done these last months if I hadn't been keeping that boy's mind occupied. 'Idle hands are the devil's workshop,' remember." Granny's face is all pinchy. "I'm more than a little surprised that incident with the ax didn't knock half of Stanley's brains out." She peers at Mama over her spectacles. "We both know that boy can't afford to lose any brains."

I close my eyes, at least most of the way, and roll my eyeballs.

"You're right, Mother. You were, and are, a Godsend. But Stan and I don't need a man right now. We'll be fine."

Truer words have never been spoken.

"And if you don't approve and would like your money back . . ." Mama holds out the wad of cash.

Granny ignores her. "You will agree that he needs to be in school. Education is important."

"Of course! He's too smart not to be in school," Mama agrees.

Truer words have never been spoken. Except, wait. School?

"And college . . . ," Granny prods.

"That's the plan."

Whose plan is this?

"And a man would definitely help facilitate this. Why, Archibald Crutchley is an educated . . ."

"Mr. Crutchley is a fine man, Mother, but you picked my first husband, and I will be picking my last. Plus, he might be a little too refined for my taste." And with that, Mama kisses Granny on the cheek and returns to the kitchen to finish preparing tomorrow's breakfast.

I peek at Granny. Her evil scheme to keep me from the river drive has apparently worked. But we're not packed up just yet.

My head spins with ways to foil her dastardly plan to ruin my future and stand in the way of my destiny. Unfortunately, my head is also spinning because I'm dizzy again and because I'm tired. Last night I heard terrible howls, a reminder of the wild creatures that live in the surrounding woods.

I will not admit to a soul that my death-defying accident with the ax or my wariness of howling creatures has left me slightly under the weather, but as I scoot out of the bottom bunk, I stumble a little. Granny rushes to steady me.

"Stanley Slater!" she barks, shaking her head. "I knew it was too soon after your accident to be bouncing around like nothing has happened. You need rest, my child." She acts like my brush with death was my fault.

Also, I am not her child. And rest is for mama's boys. And I am quite obviously not one of those.

Granny steadies me as I climb into the top bunk. I slink my covers up and my feet down to the bottom of the mattress, where my toes touch the hairy stubble of something cold. I scream like a little girl, I am not afraid to say it. It's either the head of a frozen lumberjack or the head of a frozen loup-garou, but either way, it's not good.

Granny jolts like a snake bit her, and Mama runs in with Aunt Lois and Geri right behind. I glare at all of them.

"There. Is. Something. Hairy. And. Frozen. IN. MY. BED!" My knees are drawn up all the way to my chest and I am scrunched in the corner, as far away from the terrifying head as I possibly can be. Geri doesn't even try to hide her guilt; she starts laughing then and there. Granny reaches under my covers with a smile and pulls out a frozen, dead raccoon.

"Never a dull moment," she says with a smirk and a wink at Mama.

"Is that the raccoon the shanty boys snuck into Hoot Mitchum's bunk last night?" Aunt Lois asks, peering more closely.

"Could be." Granny nods as she pitches the dead animal into the night. She is laughing, Aunt Lois is laughing, and even Mama is laughing.

I'm disgusted. "Geri," I hiss, "when you least expect it, expect it!" I roll over to go to sleep. Mama reaches up and rubs my shoulders, slow circles that could calm a savage beast, while those villainous, tickle-brained pignuts cackle their way back to the kitchen.

I plot my revenge, but I dream about bacon and wanigans.

CHAPTER 26

It is certainly not in my nature to question a man's character. Even if that character isn't as bad as what you used to think that character was.

I am a whiz at judging character, I don't mind saying.

But when a certain someone whose name rhymes with "inky feet" sits down on the bench beside you, it is nothing less than a life-or-death situation. I am a mouse stalked by a cat. I am a hen, and he is the fox. Stinky Pete is not a person I need or want to know. He always tries to talk to me when we play cribbage, when he helps me peel potatoes, or when he ruffles my hair and tells me he thinks I've grown a foot in the last few months. He asks about my day, what I like to do, how my mama is doing. What does he want from me?

And he should stop asking questions about my mama. He's about as interesting as a slice of bread.

"Huh?" Stinky Pete says as he galumphs his big self down. "Did you say something?"

"Um," I answer through my teeth, "I said, 'I have known a catcher named Fred.'" I am going to keep this conversation short and sweet. Or at least short.

Fred

"Oh! How did I not know you're a fellow baseball fan? Who's your favorite player?"

The last thing I'm trying to do is engage a man of Stinky Pete's reputation in casual conversation.

Actually, the last thing I'm trying to do is inhale through my nose. The guy did not earn that name for nothing.

"SHERLOCK HOLMES"

Probably doesn't play baseball.

"Well." I scratch around my brain for a name. I am not a follower of baseball, let's be honest. "Well, I am a big fan of Sherlock Holmes!" I immediately realize my mistake, but it's too late, and someone named Stinky Pete probably doesn't read much anyway.

"You mean, the detective in the Arthur Conan Doyle books?" Stinky Pete stares at me with a puzzled look.

"Um, no, the other one! The catcher for the Chicago Colts?" I wince and hold my breath. I do know that's a real team, at least. Uncle Henry can't stop talking about them.

"Hmmm. Can't say as I'm familiar with him." He scratches his head. "And I thought I knew all the players on that team. There's Malachi Kittridge and Cap Anson and Pop Schriver . . ."

I interrupt before he goes through the whole lineup. "Well, enough about me. Who is your favorite?"

Before I know it, I am having a conversation with a known killer. And even worse than that, a guy who is sweet on my mama.

"I'm a pretty big fan of Jimmy Ryan, although I understand why so many people love Cap Anson. Hard to argue with his averages. I went to a game last summer at West Side Grounds. One of the best nights of my life."

I change the subject before he goes into a reenactment of the entire game. The guy loves his baseball, that's for sure.

But I have other plans for my day.

"Oh, sorry for talking your ear off," Stinky Pete says with a wink. He sits back suddenly with a grin. "You go ahead and get those plans under way. I like to take a few minutes to myself each day, anyway."

Stinky Pete reaches down into his boot and pulls out a little slip of paper, yellowed and crinkly. I am completely not interested in what's on that piece of paper, but my eyeballs just can't help glancing in that direction.

I scoot a little closer. Stinky Pete unfolds the paper carefully, and a tiny bit falls into the dirty snow at our feet. His big sausage fingers smooth a crease and he silently mouths the words in front of him:

It's never too late to be what you might have been.

Stinky Pete has his elbows on his knees and is stooped forward like his shoulders are holding up the entire sky. He twists his massive neck to look at me. "Not a bad motto, don't you think?" he asks.

I nod. I can't seem to help myself, because it might not be too late to be a man, but it is becoming clear it very well might be too early. The river drive. Fathers. Manly manhood. They are so far ahead of me, it's like looking through the wrong end of a telescope.

"I want to be a lumberjack," I blurt. This guy has a way of weaseling into a fellow's skull and making him spit out his brains.

He is so sneaky.

"But I don't think I'll ever get a chance to be who I want to be."

Stinky Pete leans against the wall. He stretches his legs, looks down at his paper, and says, "Seems to me you're young enough that the whole world is before you. No regrets, no mistakes, nothing but possibility."

"Huh," I scoff. "You don't know my granny."

"Cora?" Stinky Pete asks with a grin. "Sweet little Cora? I'll tell you something—there's more to that woman than meets the eye."

"You must be thinking of someone else."

Stinky Pete folds his arms behind his head, closes his eyes, and smiles. "So I'm a pretty good listener. You know, I used to be a preach—"

"Killer? Yeah. I know. But your secret is safe with me." And the fourteen other people I told.

Stinky Pete opens his eyes. He is obviously shocked I know his secret. "Well, that's not exactly what I was going to say. . . ."

"Granny and Mama won't let me go on the river drive," I say. "They think it's dangerous and something bad will happen to me. Geri can go, and if I had a father, a real honest-to-gosh father, I could go. But I don't. So I'm being shipped to some town to go back to school." This guy is really, really good at getting a fellow to spill his guts.

"Hmmm," he replies.

"And I just don't want to! I'm this close to going to the river drive," I say, my pointer finger and thumb a hairbreadth apart. Because I really am that close. There's less and less snow every day, the ice on the river is now only a jagged edge on the banks, and I don't have to turn on my kerosene lamp to read until Mama and Granny crawl into their bunk.

"Interesting," Stinky Pete says. "Well, I'm a firm believer in honoring your mother and father."

"What about honoring your granny?" I ask. "Do I have to do that, too?"

"Well, I have to think she probably has your best interests in mind," Stinky Pete replies. His head rests against the building, his eyes are shut, and he's smiling. "And she's not nearly as bad as you think, so I'd say honor your granny as well."

The door slams and we both jump to high Heaven.

"Stanley Arthur Slater, I believe I was very clear in my instructions that until you stop feeling faint in the head, you will be parking yourself in our room, at the table, or in your bunk, and focusing your efforts on activities that are decidedly not physical." Granny's hand clenches a carving knife, and her eyes burn over the rims of her spectacles.

I slowly get up from the bench. Stinky Pete gives me a salute, and Granny grabs my ear, the tender part at the top, mind you, and drags me to my doom.

I am trapped in our room until the Good Lord raptures our souls, I reckon.

Honor your granny.

That's the last time I take advice from someone with "stinky" in his name.

CHAPTER 27

P*ssst!*" Geri whispers. "Get up!" She happens to be the loudest whisperer in the history of whisperers.

I raise myself up on an elbow and wipe the sleep from my eyes. "What are you doing here?" I ask groggily. It's possible this is a dream. Or a nightmare, depending on what happens next.

"You need to get out of here," Geri whispers from the back door.

Suddenly I feel wide-awake. "Why? What's happened? Has a loup-garou been spotted? Is someone coming to kill me?" I yelp.

"No, you chowderhead." Geri snorts. "I need some excitement, and you need some fresh air. Doctor's orders. The last of the men left the cook shanty about five minutes ago, so we have an hour before your mama and Granny come to check on you. *Come on!*" she says, her eyes an intense blue even in the dim light of our cabin.

I climb unsteadily from the bunk, throw on my coat and hat, and follow Geri outside, her half-buttoned coat trailing behind her like it's trying to keep up.

"I'm dying," I say to her as we sneak out. I really don't feel well, and although Geri is not known for her accurate medical advice, I really have nowhere else to turn; Granny will confine me to bed for all my livelong days, or at least until I'm twenty-two, and there won't even be any hope Mama will reconsider her stance on the river drive.

"Leave the diagnosing to me, please," Geri replies.

"No, really, I feel dizzy. Mama says I have dark circles under my eyes. I constantly crave bacon. These unending days of isolation are taking their toll," I plead with her.

Geri stops and looks at me. "You've been in that room for no more than two hours. One, if you count the hour you spent on the porch with poor Mr. McLachlan. So stop with the dramatics." She takes off and I have to jog to keep up. "If you have anything," she yells over her shoulder, "it's tedium!"

"Tedium?" This sounds serious. "How much longer do I have to live?"

"Hard to say," Geri answers. "Now, I have been bottled up in that cook shanty for months. I think it's time to finally have a little fun."

I have flashbacks to October and the leaf fire behind the house but tag along behind her anyway. "Look, is tedium deadly? Is there a cure for it? Is there any hope for me?"

"Well," Geri says, "there's no hope for you, but there is a cure for tedium, sometimes referred to as acute boredom, and I'm about to show you what it is." We near the outhouses, a place I usually avoid since the smell alone makes a man question his need to go to the bathroom.

"It's in an outhouse?" I can't imagine a worse cure. I might rather die.

"Here's the plan," Geri says. She has pulled to a stop and is staring at the empty outhouse nearest to us. "We're going to tip this baby over." Her eyes gleam in the dusky light.

"Are you kidding me?" I hiss. Of all the featherbrained ideas, this takes the cake. But I can tell it's too late—there's no stopping Geri when she's got an idea in her head. It reminds me of the time she talked me into walking out on the ice in the harbor because it was "as solid as a rock." Of course, I fell in and she didn't.

She parks her feet behind the outhouse and pushes and rocks and pushes the wooden structure with all her might.

"Hey!" a voice hollers from inside. I widen my eyes in shock. There's a person in there! "Hey! What's going on?" the voice yells again. But rather than frightening Geri, the fact that someone is in the outhouse seems to be encouraging her. And I recognize that voice. It's Mr. Crutchley. My sworn enemy.

Geri stops pushing for a moment. "Since when is Mr. Crutchley your sworn enemy," she whispers.

"Since now," I say. And since I overheard Granny's evil plan to have him marry Mama. I start pushing on that outhouse with all my might.

"Hey! Hey!" Mr. Crutchley yells. "Stop! I'm in here!"

We keep rocking the outhouse until the entire thing flops over onto its front, plopping down smack-dab on the door, trapping that horrible excuse for a man inside the privy until the cows come home. Hopefully with his pants around his ankles.

Geri grabs my arm and hauls me toward the cook shanty, shaking with laughter. We slip in the door and plop down on the bottom bunk. I have not laughed this much since Conrad McAllister had Mrs. Cavanaugh's pink unmentionables on his head.

Geri wipes her teary eyes and gasps through her giggles. "Oh, Stan," she says, "you surprised me! I thought for sure you would chicken out like you usually do."

I stop laughing, because this is *not* funny. "Excuse me? Who are you calling a chicken?" I ask, pointing a finger right at her nose. "I would not mess with me, if I were you."

We can still hear Mr. Crutchley pounding on the outhouse walls, yelling for help. Geri pops up, wiggles her fingers in my direction, flips her hair, and leaves.

That girl infuriates me. I do have to admit, however, that even though she's a horrible cousin, as far as making a fellow feel better, she really is just what the doctor ordered.

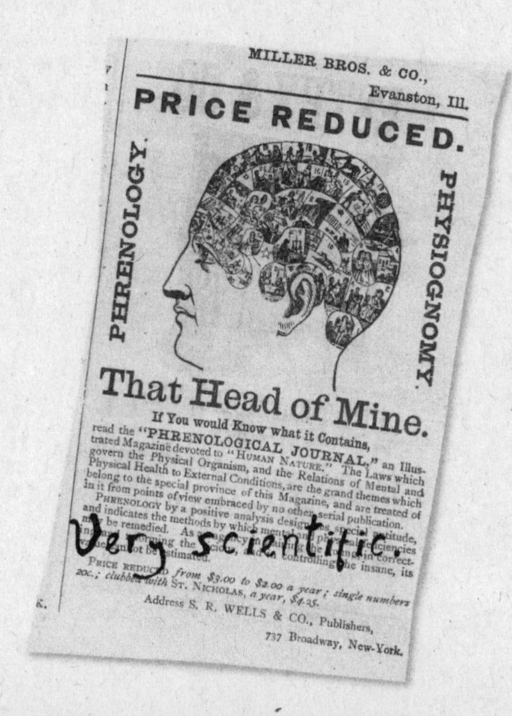

Dear Son,

Just writing to let you know I am a doctor. During my time at the sanitarium, I learned everything there is to know about doctoring and can tell you Geri doesn't know what she's talking about. She doesn't even know what effluvia is.

I'm also an expert in phrenology, the practice of examining the bumps on people's heads. This is an exact science that accurately diagnoses a person's health and personality. It has also kept me so busy I haven't had time to write. There are a lot of bumpy heads out there.

As an expert in heads, I think it's important for you to know that you have very manly bumps on your head. I can tell without even looking at them because manly head bumps run in the family.

I will be sending you some hair gel, an electric hairbrush, and a face mask for Geri. Hopefully it will help her face.

From,
Dad

I'm afraid it will tak
a lot more than this

CHAPTER 28

I am not dizzy.

I am not dizzy.

Mama feels my forehead. "How are you feeling?" she asks.

"Not dizzy, I assure you of that!" I say. The room sways like the time I stood up in Uncle Carl's boat when we were fishing.

Apparently it is a well-known rule that you're not supposed to stand up in a boat when you're fishing. This is because it can lead to possibly capsizing the boat and sinking your uncle's fishing pole, lures, and lunch box. And then you will not have any food and might be made to row the whole way back. And you'll be hungry. And wet. And your uncle Carl will be mad.

Not that I know anything about that.

Mama is folding clothes, organizing her toiletries, and putting everything into our crates. Uncle Carl should be here in the morning to take us to St. Ignace, where I will go to school, make new friends, and probably die of boredom.

"So," Mama says, looking hard at me, "you wouldn't happen to know anything about an outhouse being tipped over, would you?"

"Huh?" I ask as I burrow my nose more deeply into the pages of *Huck Finn*. "Did you say something, Mama? You *are* aware how dizzy I have been lately, right?" I place my hand against my forehead like I'm having a fainting spell.

"Mmmm-hmmm." Mama nods.

"I mean, I've not left this room except to go use the water closet. And I haven't seen anyone for weeks. Mr. Crutchley, especially. Because I really, um, wouldn't want him trapped in an outhouse or anything."

Mama drops the magazines she's holding and they fall onto the table with a thump. She grabs *Huck Finn* and throws it on my bunk. Then she grabs my hand, pulls me up until I'm standing, and marches me into the kitchen.

"This," she says through her teeth, "is *not* acceptable behavior."

"But, but!" I protest. "It was all Geri's idea!" Geri is at

the sink, peeling potatoes. She looks quickly in my direction, glares, and points the potato peeler at me.

I am not afraid of a potato peeler. I am not a potato.

"Geri." Mama stops short of the door. "Is this true?"

Geri turns to Mama and bats her eyelashes. "Why, Aunt Alice, I hope you know I could never do anything like tip over an outhouse." She gives a charming little laugh. "Oh, I'm too petite and delicate for that. And," she continues, "I could never, ever do anything to possibly hurt a fellow human being. Especially dear Mr. Crutchley." She nods and bats her lashes some more as I glare at her behind Mama's back.

Mama tilts her head and smiles at Geri, patting her cheek. "I'm sorry I doubted you, dear," she says, then squeezes my hand and pulls me out the front door.

I turn around to look behind me and Geri is leaning against the doorway, smirking.

"But, but!" I protest.

"But nothing, Stanley. Trying to blame all of this on your sweet cousin." Mama sniffs.

"But—but it was *her* idea!" I sputter.

"Listen, son." Mama stops in the road right outside the van and makes me look her in the eye. "Men do not blame others for things they bring upon themselves. They take responsibility for their actions. Now *you* are going to take responsibility and apologize to Mr. Crutchley."

She stomps up the stairs, pulling me along. Through the door I spy Mr. Crutchley behind the counter with Uncle Henry.

"Get in here. Now," Mama says, opening the door. As soon as Uncle Henry sees us enter, he makes a beeline for the back room. Mr. Crutchley grins as he spies Mama, but the grin quickly loses its shine when he sees me.

"Oh, hello, Stan." His mouth says hello and the smile stays on his face, but his eyes say, "You have killed my pet chicken and eaten its innards. I will avenge its death!"

"I have not killed your pet chicken or eaten its innards, Mr. Crutchley," I clarify.

Mama and Mr. Crutchley look at each other and then at me.

"Um, Mr. Crutchley, Stanley is here to apologize." Mama squeezes my shoulder and pushes me forward. Mr. Crutchley leans against the counter, his arms folded tightly across his chest. He looks like he's waiting for something.

"Stan! He *is* waiting for something," Mama says crossly.

Mr. Crutchley smiles at her sadly; then he stands straight and says, "Alice, let me make this easier on the both of you." He nods sympathetically and places a hand on my shoulder. "Obviously this is a boy who needs a man around. Otherwise I'm sure he's destined for a life of delinquency and crime."

Mama's mouth is slightly open and her head tilts to the side.

Mr. Crutchley puts out a hand to hold Mama's wrist. "Let me take care of this," he reassures her. "I'll just grab a switch from the willow by the river. A few hard swats will be a good reminder of how we expect Stanley to behave."

Mama frowns and shakes her head like she's brushing cobwebs from her brain; then she wrenches her wrist from

Mr. Crutchley's hand and drags me out of the van, spitting words as she leads me to the cook shanty.

"Can you believe the nerve?" she says, marching down the road. I have to jog to keep up with her or risk having my arm pulled from its socket. "Am I doing such a poor job raising this child on my own that everyone and his brother seems to think they have to give me advice?"

I glance behind me at the van. Mr. Crutchley looks a bit like a lost puppy, staring from the doorway.

I smile at him because I won this little battle. If Mama has to choose between Mr. Crutchley or me, it's pretty apparent who the winner is.

Geri.

"Is everything okay, Aunt Alice?" she asks as we stumble into the kitchen. "Dear Stan, are you all right?" Her voice is so sticky sweet that if you tipped her over, syrup would pour from her mouth.

"Yes, dear," Mama says, and she drops my arm with a sigh, pats Geri's shoulder, and heads to the sink to wash her hands for the dinner prep.

Geri grins at me. "Did you get in trouble?" she whispers.

"No," I answer. "But no thanks to you."

"Oh, I knew it would be okay," she says with a wink. "Plus, if your mama marries Mr. Crutchley, you two will have to get along. This was a good test!" she adds cheerily.

What? First Granny, now Geri. Mr. Crutchley? My father? Why do people keep thinking this is an option?

"Well, he'd be a good provider," Geri says with a shrug. "And he dresses nicely. And your mother looked quite taken with him yesterday when he presented her with Mr. Mark Twain's most recent novel."

This is the worst news I've heard since Granny arrived at our door. Seems like Mr. Crutchley found the key to Mama's heart—she's a sucker for a good book.

Geri thinks he's the key to my finally getting to the river drive, but I'm not so sure it's worth the price I'll have to pay.

Dear Son,

I will soon be returning from whaling in the Arctic. I have caught four whales with just my bare hands and some peanuts.

I will be sending you a polar bear, ivory tusks, a glacier, and a narwhal.

Do not tell Geri. She would want her very own

polar bear, and I'm not sure she won't kill it with some deadly disease.

Just wait a little longer. And keep your sweet mama away from the dastardly villain whose name rhymes with Mr. Cat Flea. He is almost as evil as your granny.

Your Explorer of a Father,
Dad

Quiet murmurs cause me to look up from my father's letter. Although I'm not known to overreact, the scene before me is stranger than two cats on a swing.

Copyright by Frees. THE BUFKINS TWINS WERE SWINGING.

Stinky Pete. And Granny. Peering in my direction and whispering.

After the incident in the bunkhouse, they may not be sworn enemies, but they certainly aren't best friends. This can only mean one thing.

The world is ending.

Or Stinky Pete wants me severely punished for beating him at cribbage last night. Again.

I am a whiz at cribbage, I don't mind saying.

"Alice," Granny says, "change of plans."

Mama wipes her floury hands on her apron as she approaches the devilish duo.

"What's that?" she asks.

"Well," Granny explains, looking over at me but not lowering her voice. In fact, her tone sounds more like a warning. "Peter has offered to watch after Stanley during the river drive." She waits for Mama's response, but Mama is frozen to the spot.

Stinky Pete winks at me.

"But, Mother," Mama argues, "you were the one who rejected the idea in the first place! And I agreed! The river drive is much, much too dangerous for Stan. You saw what happened with the ax."

What is the big deal? Men often have accidents with sharp things. It's how the mama's boys are weeded out.

"And he didn't even pick *up* the ax. Imagine what could happen near water. And with peaveys."

That word still makes me cringe.

"And logjams and dynamite."

Well, chop off my legs and call me Shorty! Did she say "dynamite"? This day has definitely taken a turn for the better.

CHAPTER 29

Stinky Pete grins at Mama, who is sputtering and carrying on like a train barreling down a track.

"Now, ma'am, Mrs. Slater, he'll be fine. I promise I will keep an eye on Stan and won't let anything bad happen to him."

Mama looks at him skeptically and starts to erupt. Stinky Pete backs up against the table.

"You!" She pokes him in the chest. "This is your idea? Like you think you know what's best for my son?"

He looks at Mama like everything she says is a sweet melody but holds his hands up in a "Not me!" gesture.

Granny pipes up. "No, Alice, it was my idea."

Which is more than slightly suspicious, but also lowers that woman's Evil Rating to a solid 72.6 percent.

"What?" Mama screeches. Geri stops her potato peeling and glances at me in shock.

I have to admit, my mama does not usually act like someone has wound her up like an eight-day clock.

Granny continues without an apology. "Listen, you are not quite financially ready for this next step, even with the extra money I've been saving." Granny puts an arm around Mama's angry shoulders. "You need the money, Henry needs more cooks, and Stanley will be kept occupied so you don't have to worry about him. It's only logical."

Mama spouts off something about my being "accident-prone" and a "menace to all around."

I am just about sure that Butch Cassidy's mama would never call him "accident-prone." Although, as an outlaw, he probably *is* a menace to all around.

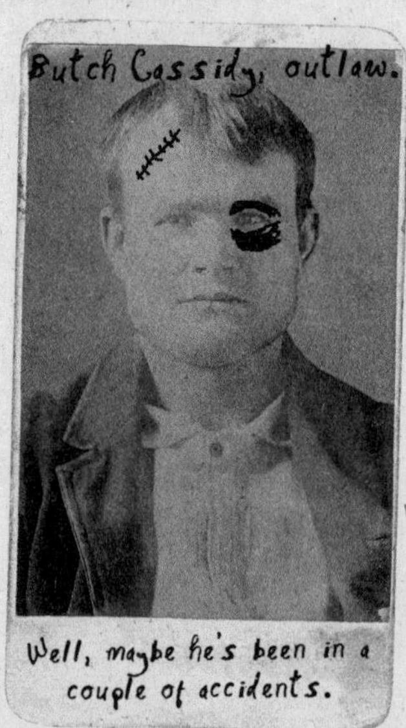

Dear Son,

I'm an outlaw. I'm not guilty but am very dangerously brave and devilishly handsome. So you understand why you have these very same traits.

It is a burden to be so handsome and brave. And smart. And good at dominoes and cribbage.

After I rustle me some horses and rob a train or two, I will come save you from the crazy people who do not appreciate your talents. Then I will settle down and become a law-abiding citizen—perhaps even a sheriff.

Do not tell Geri. She is not to be trusted. She cheats at dominoes, and I'm pretty sure she would have me arrested.

From,
Dad

Geri sidles up to me. I cover my letter, an unnecessary move since her attention seems to be elsewhere. "What has gotten into your mama?" she asks, glancing in Mama's direction. And then she says, "Aw, do you see Mr. McLachlan? The way he looks at Aunt Alice, it's like he's got his heart on his sleeve."

"What do you mean his heart is on his sleeve? You need to get over there right now and take care of that, missy! This is a major medical emergency!" I pull on her arm, but she shakes it loose.

"Stan, it's just an expression. It means he likes her."

"Of course I knew that," I scoff. Actually, I did *not* know that, but it's true that Stinky Pete is gazing at Mama with a twinkle in his eye.

He is even more dangerous than I thought. Maybe even more dangerous than Mr. Crutchley.

Mama's dull roar has quieted down. For now it seems like she's just giving Stinky Pete a laundry list of ways to keep me safe. "Under no terms is he to leave your sight." Stinky Pete nods. "Nor will he be handling anything sharp," she says as she pokes him in the chest.

What is the sense of a man going on the river drive unless he can handle something sharp?

"Remember," she reminds Stinky Pete, looking him square in the eye, "this is a child who hurt himself simply looking at an ax."

Stinky Pete nods. Granny nods. Mama's face softens.

If Mama has her way, I'll be tied to the shore like a dog on a leash.

This is not quite the river drive I had in mind.

CHAPTER 30

I want to be very clear," Mama says. "You being on this river drive is against my better judgment, so the minute you get yourself into the slightest bit of danger, we are on a wagon to St. Ignace."

I'm an expert on danger and handling the river, I don't mind saying. I've been getting buckets of water from it for months—we're practically on a first-name basis. But I let her cool off a little and stay near the cook shanty for a few days until even she gets tired of having me underfoot.

"Go outside. But stay away from trouble," she warns.

As if I would ever get in trouble.

I meander around camp, innocently hoping to find ways

to prove my skills with both logs and water. Unfortunately, even if your mama says you are allowed to go on the river drive, it doesn't mean you jump on a log and become immediately famous for your natural logrolling abilities. Apparently debris has to be cleaned out of the rivers and along the paths to the rivers while the waters continue to swell with melting snow and bitter rain. No one tells you about that humdrum part of the river drive.

Some of the lumberjacks leave when the work in the woods is done to make way for the river pigs. Hoot and Knut and Cager all wave goodbye, pay in hand.

And I'm still not out on that river.

Of course Mr. Crutchley is still here.

And Stinky Pete.

The bad ones never leave.

Stinky Pete has had his twinkly eyes on me. All the time.

For example, one day last week I simply wanted to light a little match to start a fire in Cooter's blacksmith shop. Just to see how hot the fire could get. And maybe try my hand at a little blacksmithy kind of work, just to see if I'm a natural.

I'm pretty sure I'm a natural.

Guess who kept coming up behind me to blow out the match as soon as I got it lit?

That's right. Stinky Pete and his bad breath and twinkly eyes.

"Stan . . . ," he said. But I ran off before he could carry

on about how great the Chicago White Stockings were when he was a kid.

Then yesterday I approached an ax leaning against the van, the one gleaming in the sun, the one I was not even going to touch, just simply examine for possible bloodstains from my violent accident, when Stinky Pete ran over from the bunkhouse, snatched the ax from my hand like it was a twig fallen from a tree, shook a finger at me, and winked.

"Stan . . . ," he said. But I ran off before he could carry on about quotes and the meaning of life.

And just today I ran down to check out the river pigs preparing the logs for the river drive. The water rushed by like it couldn't wait to be filled with men and logs and salty language. Every time I hear it or see it, my heart speeds up to match its roar.

Some of the men are building wanigans for the cooks to follow the river pigs with hot cooked meals. I will be spending most of my time on one of these boats and want to get my two cents' worth in.

Plus, I am a whiz at building, I don't mind saying.

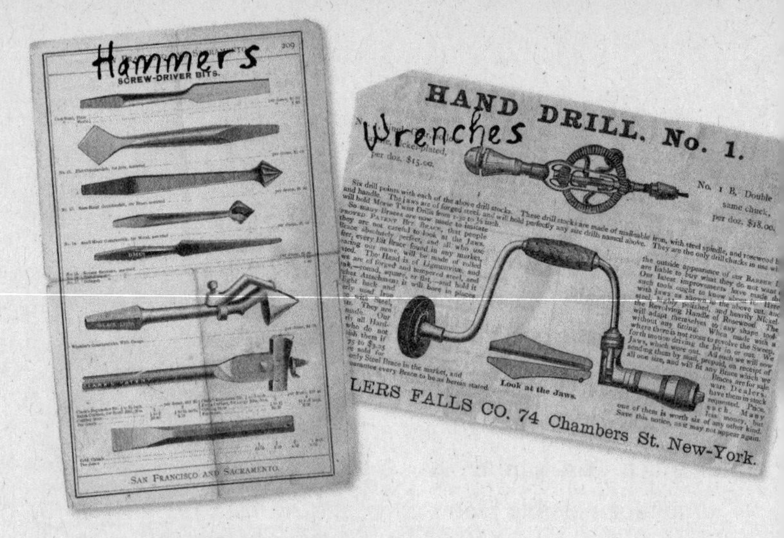

So I meandered down to the water, and lo and behold, there was Stinky Pete, barreling behind me like a bull after a matador. So I took off running, zigzagging around stumps and over logs, so fast I was a blur, as fast as Frank Goodale when he rode Chant in last year's Kentucky Derby.

I ran and ran and I never ran out of breath. I ran and

ran and I never ran out of speed. I ran and ran. And suddenly I did run out of land.

And ended up smack-dab in the icy river, the current pulling me like the hand of the devil himself.

Stinky Pete was right behind me, however, and fished me out with one arm and a twinkly grin.

I got the feeling he was enjoying this. And why is he always so twinkly?

"Why am I so what?" he asked me, still holding my shoulders so I couldn't escape.

"Um, I just wondered why my shirt's so wrinkly." I tugged on my collar and tried to examine it like wrinkles offend my very soul.

Stinky Pete looked at me, puzzled. Then he took a deep breath. "Stan," he said with a sigh, "I have been running after you all morning. Could you please hold on one dad-blamed minute? I want to ask you something." He let go of my shoulders and straightened himself up.

My eyes darted around to see if I could make my getaway, but I was too waterlogged to give much of a fight. I just sighed and Stinky Pete ran his fingers through his hair as he caught his breath.

"Okay. Now. I have to head down to the curve in the river and dynamite some rocks so the logs don't get caught up. I was wondering if you'd like to join me."

I stared at him. And stared some more.

Had Stinky Pete just said "dynamite"? That right there is one of my favorite words.

"Why didn't you say so?" I asked, exasperated. "It would have saved me a lot of running."

Plus, I am a whiz at the dynamite, I don't mind saying.

Stinky Pete grinned, his white teeth sparkly and twinkly in the sunlight. "I thought so," he said.

CHAPTER 31

"You do realize I'm not a murderer, right?" Stinky Pete looks at me. We are walking to the crook in the river, a stick of dynamite in Stinky Pete's hand and a box of matches in his pocket.

I wave an arm between us. "Yeah, yeah," I answer. "Whatever you want people to believe. Your secret is safe with me," I reassure him with a wink.

Stinky Pete laughs, throws an arm around me, and squeezes my shoulder. "Well, that's a relief," he says.

"Did you really kill a man?" The words spill from my mouth before I even have a chance to think about them.

Stinky Pete stops suddenly. His eyes, for once, don't

twinkle. He doesn't wink. Instead his arm drops and his hands clench, and I wish, once again, that I thought about something before I actually said it.

"Stan," he says without looking at me, "the past is the past. I can't do anything about it. So I"—he takes a deep breath—"I choose to live in the present and plan for my future. Life is short." And then he takes off and I have to jog to keep up with him.

What just happened? Did I say something? Of course I said something! I asked the exact question Uncle Henry told me not to ask. This isn't some little insult like I spurt out at Conrad McAllister. No, I think I hurt Stinky Pete, a guy who has never been anything but nice to me. Unlike Conrad McAllister, who whitewashed my face until I said he was the smartest person I knew.

By the way, just because I said it doesn't mean it's true. I was being tortured.

All Stinky Pete has ever done is play games with me or show me how to whittle or teach me to whistle all the verses of "Oh, My Darling Clementine."

I'm having trouble keeping up with him, and before I know it, just like my dad, Stinky Pete is gone.

I stop. Is that what happened with my dad? Did I run him off, too?

There's a robin poking around the ground. The running river water, loud and rushing, reminds me that I'm finally, *finally* getting to ride the river and prove I'm a man. I'll prove I can take care of my mama and that we don't need any other men, or Granny, in our lives telling us what to do. I have waited my whole, entire life for this.

But all I can think about is Stinky Pete and how he's long gone.

I plop myself onto a downed log. Even the possibility of dynamite doesn't matter to me now. Nothing matters anymore. Not the river drive. Not bacon.

Okay, maybe bacon.

I haul myself up and turn to head back to camp. Maybe there will be something to eat when I return. I can drown my sorrows in food. I start trudging through snow that seems a lot harder to tromp through than it was earlier. Of course that's when I was heading toward an explosion. Now I am just returning to some bossy women.

"Stan!" I turn to see Stinky Pete walking quickly toward me. "What are you doing? I thought you were right behind me."

"I'm heading back to camp," I say, not looking at him directly.

"Back to camp?" Stinky Pete scratches his head with the end of the dynamite. "Why? We haven't even set off the explosion yet."

"Well," I say quietly, "I figured you wouldn't want me to go with you now. You know, since I asked you about, well, that thing I shouldn't have asked you."

"Why would you think that?" Stinky Pete asks.

"You still want me to go with you?"

"Why wouldn't I?" he says. "You're my partner in crime!" Stinky Pete stoops to my height. "I guess I forgot to tell you," he says, laying his large hand on my shoulder. "When someone knows life is short, they also know what's important. And what's important to me is spending time with my favorite people, one of whom is you." He messes up my hat and stands. "Now c'mon. Let's do this job so we can get going on the river drive."

Exactly! I will soon have the chance to show the world my natural logrolling talent. My insides suddenly feel puffed up with air and I'm as light-footed as a cat. I follow Stinky Pete thrashing through the brush.

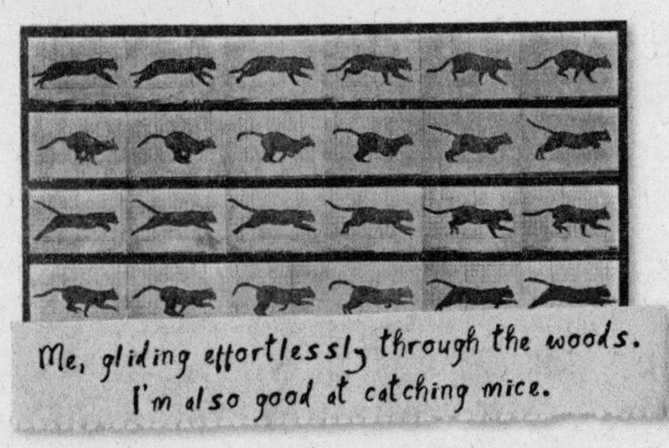

Me, gliding effortlessly through the woods.
I'm also good at catching mice.

"Stan, I saw you stand on the log we use for chopping firewood over by the bunkhouse. No offense, but your sense of balance could use some improvement," Stinky Pete says.

"You are so wrong," I reply, offended. "I have been practicing nonstop and am now a whiz at balancing, I don't mind saying."

"Well, you fell five times yesterday alone, so I'm hoping you don't have any foolish ideas floating around in that head of yours," Stinky Pete says, glancing back with his twinkly eyes.

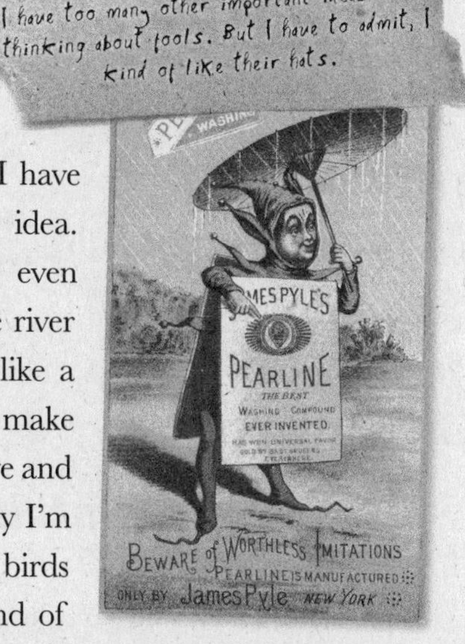

Oh, how I missed those twinkly eyes. It has been so long since I last saw them.

Also, I am just about sure I have never entertained a foolish idea. Plus, how am I supposed to even get a chance to practice on the river if Stinky Pete is watching me like a hawk? He keeps checking to make sure I'm right behind him. I wave and give him a thumbs-up, but really I'm lollygagging a bit. I listen to the birds chirp in the trees and the sound of the rushing water and the yells from the river pigs. I am lost in my thoughts when I hear a squeaky voice off in the distance.

"Stanley!" It sounds like someone is calling my name.

"Stanley!" I hear again. I turn around and who should I see tiptoeing through the forest in his fancy trousers, white shirt, and suspenders but Mr. Crutchley.

He scampers up to me, all out of breath. "What, young man, are you doing here alone and unsupervised?"

"I'm here to make sure Stinky Pete sets off the dynamite correctly," I reply.

Stinky Pete has jogged back to us. He looks at me and grins.

Mr. Crutchley regains his breath and swats me away like a pesky fly.

"So, Peter," he says, limply slapping Stinky Pete on the shoulder, "I thought I'd check out the operation here so I can give a report to the boss." He stomps through the woods without giving me a second thought. Stinky Pete glances at me and wriggles an eyebrow. He nods as Mr. Crutchley informs him how both dynamite and a ten-year-old boy should be handled.

"I'm almost twelve!" I shout. Mr. Crutchley doesn't even

listen, but Stinky Pete gives me a smile from behind his back.

We pass a roll-away of logs along the riverbank, ready to be dumped into the roiling water. I imagine riding those logs: I will run across them, hoot and holler, all the river pigs will hoot and holler, and people on the banks of the main river will hoot and holler and tell stories of my feats for generations to come.

I pause next to one very large pile, ready to scale it and get this show on the road, when a hand clamps down on my shoulder.

"Stanley Slater! Don't even think about it! This is how people get killed! You simply jostle one wrong log and the entire stack will come tumbling down upon you, and you are flat as a pancake and killed." Mr. Crutchley purses his lips and shakes his finger.

"Peter, this is what I was talking about," he says. "The boy is simply not to be trusted."

Stinky Pete pushes me away from the logs and doesn't stop pushing me until we're far from the temptation of my destiny.

"He needs to leave this camp full of hooligans and ne'er-do-wells, and I am certainly the only one to provide him with that opportunity." Mr. Crutchley blows about like a stiff winter gale, his tiny lips pursed in disapproval and his long pointy nose sticking out from under the brim of his hat like the head of a rat.

Stinky Pete burrows himself into his collar, punches his hands deep in his pockets, and barrels ahead like he's walking into the wind. He just nods as Mr. Crutchley blathers on.

"When Alice accepts my hand in marriage, I will be able to provide for her son as well," he says. I whip my head up just as Stinky Pete's neck seems to disappear into his coat. He doesn't say a word, but I'm starting to realize something.

"There's a fine military academy in Indiana where Stanley will learn manners and discipline. They will teach him how to conduct himself as a proper young gentleman before he starts his military career."

Stinky Pete throws branches into the river as if they have offended the good name of his mother, and the wild current whips them up like butter in a churn.

And then suddenly it becomes clear. As clear as the water of Lake Michigan in June.

Mr. Crutchley is Granny. Only worse.

And Granny in comparison is only 56.7 percent evil.

Dear Son,

I have joined the circus as a strong man. I am such a strong man I am able to beat up anyone who might even consider sending you to a boring school in Indiana. You should not have to go to school. Or learn manners. Or practice discipline. No one needs to know that stuff.

All of that is for weak mama's boys who wear suspenders and don't know enough to roll up their pants while trekking through soggy marshes.

I beat those guys up most days before breakfast.

But don't tell Geri. She'll also want to join the circus, but we can't use her unless she has four legs or a beard. Or preferably both.

From,
Dad

Mr. Crutchley on his little tippy toes.

CHAPTER 32

The rock juts out of the river like Granny's crochet hook, ready to snag anything in its path. Stinky Pete wades in, dynamite in hand, the long wick held above the water, while Mr. Crutchley shouts directions like he knows what he's talking about. He tiptoes over the wet ground in an attempt to get closer to the raging water.

"Over more to the right! Don't get the wick wet! You'll need to be careful!" The river roars like a bear waking up from a winter's nap. I am pretty sure Stinky Pete can't hear a word, which means I'm on my own. With Mr. Crutchley. He glares at me, standing right beside him. "Don't move an inch, young man," he warns. "This is the work of men, not boys with no common sense. I haven't the foggiest notion why Peter McLachlan thought you needed to join us in this endeavor. You are sure to be a nuisance." He points a warning finger at me and continues shouting at Stinky Pete. I stuff my hands in my pockets and watch Stinky Pete wade to shore, hanging the long wick over low-lying branches.

"That looks good!" Mr. Crutchley yells. Stinky Pete winds his way forward, looks in our direction, and holds up three fingers. Three seconds and he will light the fuse and blow the rock to smithereens.

"Don't move," Mr. Crutchley warns again. We're right on the shore, a safe distance from the dynamite. Does he really think I'm going to run over to that rock and jump on it?

I might be brave and handsome and dangerous, but I am no fool.

Stinky Pete lights the fuse and runs toward us, head down, weaving through the branches, stumps, and trees, covering his ears. I watch the lit end of the fuse snake its way toward the rock. Mr. Crutchley jumps up and down, as excited as a little girl with a new doll.

"Oh! Dear me!" he yelps.

I am standing like the mast of a ship. Tall and straight. If

ROSIE BUFKINS GAVE JENNIE AN AIRING.

I've seen one explosion, I've seen a hundred. They're all the same. A loud boom, a blast of water, a . . .

The noise is so loud I spring up from the earth like a tightly wound jack-in-the-box.

I wave my arms and thrash around, the river close to my feet, churning and bubbling, a whirlpool of menacing water, ready to claim another body, leaving only my boots as a memento of my time here on earth.

My shoulder grazes Mr. Crutchley's hip. The earth seems less solid, less secure, more like a pitching swell, and as my feet dive forward, I reach to grab on to the only thing that might save me, even if it's the devil himself.

And Mr. Crutchley spins and spins into the bubbling abyss of churning water.

"Yeeoow!" he hollers as he tumbles headlong into the river.

I stop myself from following him by grabbing a willow branch on the bank. Stinky Pete takes hold of my wrist, pulls me up, dumps me on the ground, and makes a beeline down the shore for Mr. Crutchley, who is being swept away like a dry leaf in a tornado. I follow closely behind, weaving through the poky branches, slogging through the wet earth as Mr. Crutchley's pinhead bobs up and sputters through the foamy, cold river.

"We have to hurry and get him out!" Stinky Pete calls to me, trusting I'm right on his heels. "He'll freeze in there for sure! Run ahead! I'm pretty sure there's a curve in the river where we can reach him!" I run past the both of them. Stinky Pete cuts down a long branch with his jackknife and Mr. Crutchley raises his arms in the angry water and pleads for help.

I run up ahead a bit farther and sure enough there's a narrower stretch where we just might be able to reach Mr. Crutchley from shore.

Mr. Crutchley, who wants to marry my sweet mama.

Mr. Crutchley, who is more evil than my granny.

Mr. Crutchley, who wanted to hit me with a switch.

Mr. Crutchley, who wants to send me to a boring military school.

Would someone please remind me why I might want to save him?

I stand on the shore, frozen. Stinky Pete's mouth is saying something, but I can't hear him because of the roar in my ears. Mr. Crutchley is being swept right toward me, his head bouncing around like a crab apple in a barrel of water, and it makes my ears feel full.

Do you think we could maybe throw him back?

Stinky Pete runs toward the shore, panicked, his branch inches from Mr. Crutchley's grasp. I barely see Mr. Crutchley's fingers reach out and clasp the branch as the icy water bubbles around him. Stinky Pete plants his feet firmly, ready to reel in Mr. Crutchley like a prize trout, when the branch springs back, Mr. Crutchley's arms bounce up, his head goes under, and the whole world stops breathing.

Stinky Pete stands on the shore, motionless, the branch still in both of his hands, and stares at the last place we saw Mr. Crutchley's head before it was folded into the frothy river like egg whites in Aunt Lois's lemon pie. I shut my eyes to say a prayer for Mr. Crutchley's soul.

And to think a little about lemon pie.

"Stan!" My eyes immediately open and I see Stinky Pete pointing toward the river. Mr. Crutchley's head is above water and seems to be gaining speed as he

I need some lemon pie. Or my life is no longer worth living.

barrels toward me. I'm hypnotized by his bouncing head, the foamy water, the icy spray hitting my face. And I'm stuck to the shore.

Mr. Crutchley gets closer.

And closer.

"Stan!" Stinky Pete hollers again, running toward me. He will be too late with his branch, but I might just be able to grab Mr. Crutchley.

I can almost hear his sputters. I imagine the fear in his eyes, the chill running through his veins.

And I can't move. Except to jump up and down a little, bouncing with each bob of Mr. Crutchley's head.

I know I need to grab a branch. Or put out an arm or a leg. Or yell some encouraging words. But I'm not just watching a man fighting for his life; I'm watching my possible future heading toward me. A future that probably includes a uniform and proper manners.

Just as these thoughts float through my head like a fog, a poisonous snake drops from the tree above me. Right directly onto my left shoulder. I stand stock-still, waiting for it to sink its fangs into my skin.

I might have squealed a little bit.

Sometimes these things can't be helped.

I fling the snake from my shoulder with all my might—a blur of white

heading straight for Mr. Crutchley. As Stinky Pete runs toward me, closer and closer, Mr. Crutchley reaches for the snake.

It is a really long, dirty gray snake. And it perhaps slightly resembles a rope.

"Stan! Way to go!" Stinky Pete yells. I see Mr. Crutchley firmly attached to the rope, his face a stream of water and his hair oily streaks plastered to his head. "So glad you saw that old rope!"

I look up in the tree as Stinky Pete struggles to get Mr. Crutchley to shore. Above me, attached to the hemlock, is a rusty old pulley with a knot of rope attached. Someone, at some time, had used this to move their belongings from one side of the river to the other.

However, as far as I'm concerned, I saved Mr. Crutchley's life with quick thinking and a poisonous snake.

Mr. Crutchley sputters up from the river like a drowned rat, glaring at me as he tries to wipe the water off his face with his wet sleeve. He is breathless and hunched over, and Stinky Pete pounds on him to help him breathe.

"You!" Mr. Crutchley looks at me from his bent-over position, points a finger, and says again accusingly, "You!"

"Ya know, Stan," Stinky Pete says seriously, "when we get to camp, we'll have to tell your mama the truth."

I know, I know. I always tell the truth.

Even if I have to make it up.

CHAPTER 33

When we get to camp, Stinky Pete indeed feels the need to tell Mama the truth. Which is so much better than the real truth that I let him have at it as I just sit and listen.

"And next thing I knew," Stinky Pete says, hot tea in his hand, feet on the table (and Mr. Crutchley safely in the bunkhouse, changing out of his wet clothes), "old Crutchley is up to his neck in the river." He takes a sip of tea and shakes his head. "Someone should probably be in charge of keeping track of that guy." Uncle Henry, Geri, Aunt Lois, Granny, and Mama are hanging on his every word.

I am biting my nails, because I know how this story ends.

"So," Stinky Pete continues, "I grab a branch, hoping I can reach Crutchley before he is swept away and we don't find him until we reach Manistique. But before I can even get the branch primed and ready, what do I see? Stan! With an old pulley rope, flinging it out to Archie. Such quick thinking!" he says with a grin.

I return the smile because I am loving this version of my story.

"Is this true?" Geri asks, her mouth hanging open. "Are you talking about Stan?"

"The one and only," Stinky Pete says, leaning over to slap me on the back.

But before I can even enjoy the glory of my brave deed, the door to the cook shanty slams open and Mr. Crutchley thrashes into the room.

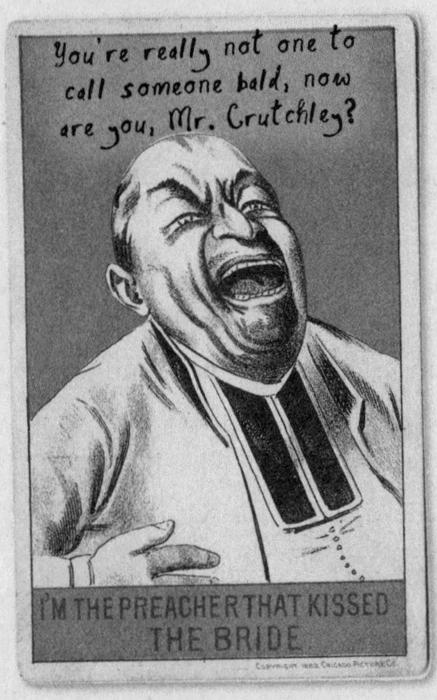

"Bald-faced liar!" Mr. Crutchley shouts, pointing an accusing finger at me.

Everyone holds his breath, except for Geri, whose head bounces between Mr. Crutchley and me like she's watching a game of lawn tennis, and Granny, whose eyes light up like the very dynamite blast that got me into this mess.

"Stanley Slater, sitting here dry and soaking in compliments like an overzealous sponge, was neither brave nor heroic. In fact, not only did he barely save me, he *pushed* me into the river to begin with!"

Mouths hang open. Geri gasps, Granny nods like this information does not surprise her, Mama's eyes look at me questioningly, and Stinky Pete shakes his head and looks down into his cup of tea.

"Well, Stan?" Uncle Henry asks sternly. "Do you care to explain?"

"Um, well . . ." I hesitate, my heart pounding in my ears.

"Yes, Stan." Mr. Crutchley's voice drips with sarcasm. "Care to explain?"

"Um." I think of all the possible stories I could tell: Mr. Crutchley falling into the river because he's not very good at balancing. Mr. Crutchley trying to push me in the river and falling in instead. Mr. Crutchley jumping in the river because his life is not worth living and then changing his mind and I save him.

Or I could run away. I could become an outlaw, or a cowboy, or an explorer. My mind reels with possibilities.

Stinky Pete sits next to me. He has taken out the piece of paper he keeps in his boot and spreads it on the table between his cup of tea and me.

It's never too late to be what you might have been.

And I pause. The door to my destiny is nearby. I could run and never come back and never again have to face Mr. Crutchley, who fully deserved to fall in the river. I could run out the door and grow a beard and spit and swear and no one would stop me. I could find my father and learn what it's like to be a man. But when I look up at Stinky Pete, a guy who is rough-and-tumble, who rarely has a harsh word for anyone, who has watched over me these last few months no matter what I've done or said, I think again. I think I might have an inkling about what makes a real man.

I take a deep breath. "It's true. It was an accident, but I did knock Mr. Crutchley into the river." Stinky Pete looks at me with a lopsided smile, his eyes warm.

"And I'm sorry. I really am sorry," I say, looking Mr. Crutchley right in the eyes.

Stinky Pete pats my knee.

"Well, sorry is not enough," Mr. Crutchley sputters. "Alice! Send the boy out to me. I am off to find a switch and teach this boy what it means to be sorry." He flings open the door and I sigh, knowing I'm going to have to take responsibility for my actions.

"Yeah, son," Stinky Pete says, "I am so proud of you for being honest and taking responsibility, but sometimes you just have to take your lumps. Part of being a man."

I start to scoot my chair from the table, but Mama stops me. "Hold it right there," she says. "I do believe what you did deserves a serious consequence, but I am still your mama and no man is going to raise a hand to my son, you hear me?"

"I'm willing to take responsibility for my actions, Mama," I reply, trying to sound braver than I actually feel.

"Well, there will be repercussions, young man, but I will be doling them out, not someone who's practically a stranger," Mama announces. "Plus, you're eleven. Hardly a man."

Why does everyone insist on reminding me?

Dear Son,

I have heard of your brave deeds and am immensely proud. While being a man has its perks (namely being able to go to bed when you want and eat like a pig), it is also important to remember that being a man also comes with responsibilities.

I think you are good and ready to think before you speak, help your mama more around the house, and not hide your flowery apron in a place it's likely to catch fire. Do not feel like you have to listen to your cousin Geri, however. That would be completely irresponsible behavior.

And if being a man means always being responsible, you might just want to avoid being a man a little while longer. "Always" might be asking a lot.

I hope to see you someday, perhaps riding a bucking bronco or accepting the keys to the city from the mayor, but in the meantime, that Stinky Pete character is not so bad. I'm not even sure he's a cold-blooded killer.

From,
Dad

Uncle Carl arrives right after breakfast the next day. He's here to give us a ride to our new diggings, because apparently when Mama mentioned "repercussions," she meant I was not going on the river drive.

"We'll just have to come up with money some other way—a way that doesn't have the possibility of someone getting hurt or dying," she said disapprovingly.

I think I would have preferred Mr. Crutchley's switch.

Our crates are packed outside the door of our room. Just my crate and turkey and Mama's crates. Granny stuffed extra magazines in my turkey in case I need some Scrapbook material.

I check the room again. Yep, Granny's things are all unpacked, minus the one stocking I still have on my left foot. When money is tight, apparently socks are not a priority, and surprisingly no one had a spare.

Or they simply enjoyed the sight of Granny's stocking on my left foot.

Granny's bed is still made, and her extra dress is hanging on the wire above the stove.

I think we've seen the last of her for a while, which is the one good thing about leaving.

Geri leans against the doorway to the kitchen, her arms folded across her chest and a smug look on her face.

"You know, I'm still going to get you back for all the pranks you pulled. Don't think I won't," I warn her.

"I have no idea what you're talking about," Geri replies. She's a liar until the bitter end, God have mercy on her soul. She helps me cart crates to the wagon, and I climb onto the seat next to Uncle Carl. Granny hands me my turkey and a little bag.

"It's your soldiers, Stan. I found them way down underneath my *Harper's Weekly*s."

I'm so glad to see these guys. I prop one on the bench next to me, the one on his knee, holding his rifle to his shoulder. He can shoot any loups-garous we encounter in the woods. That little find dropped Granny's Evil Rating to 43.5 percent. And now that it's apparent she will no longer be living with us, I feel especially generous. I will move her Evil Rating to 40.3 percent. I think the longer I go without seeing that woman, the more I'll like her.

Stinky Pete nods from the door of the cook shanty. He raises his cup as a kind of salute, while Mr. Crutchley helps Mama into the wagon.

"I'll be in town in a few weeks, Mrs. Slater. Your mother mentioned I should look in on you and Stan," he says formally.

"Oh, she did, did she?" Mama says shortly. "Well, if you must, you must."

Mr. Crutchley smiles and smooths his hair. That guy can't take a hint.

"And I'll be calling on you as well," says another, deeper voice. "If that's all right with you, Mrs. Slater."

What's this? My head swings around just in time to see

that sly dog, Stinky Pete, his twinkly eyes peering into my mama's, well, twinkly eyes. How did he get over to the wagon so fast? I might have to change his name to Sneaky Pete. And what's with all the twinkly around here?

Mama's cheeks are pink. "That would be most enjoyable, Mr. McLachlan," she replies in a low voice, smiling.

"Then it would be my pleasure," Stinky Pete says as he steps away from the wagon. He winks at me, and I do think it might be nice to see him again. He's not my dad, of course, but he's not so bad, either. After all, how many people get to say they're friends with a real, live killer?

Not that I've given up on my dad—since he could be anywhere, I'll be keeping my eyes peeled for him in St. Ignace.

"Isn't it about time to go, Uncle Carl?" I nudge him with my elbow. I want to be away from Granny and Geri and especially Mr. Crutchley as quickly as possible.

"Hold up!" Granny runs toward the wagon. She's holding a wad of something red in her left hand. "Time to return my stocking, young man."

"But my foot will get cold!" I protest. As Granny thrusts the bundle at me, I realize they are my red socks. The socks I have been missing for weeks. The missing socks that made it necessary for me to wear women's hosiery and look like a fool. I look at the socks and then at Granny. How did she get my socks? How long has she *had* my socks?

"Oh"—Granny nods matter-of-factly—"for quite some time now." The wheels in my brain tick through the last few months: The short-sheeting of my bed. The salt. The missing socks. The raccoon. Granny?

She laughs a big, hearty laugh, and everyone else starts laughing, too.

"Told you there was more to your granny than meets the eye," Stinky Pete says with a chuckle.

"She's always been the worst prankster at the lumber camp," Uncle Henry agrees. "The shanty boys never suspect her, and they always get fooled."

Granny grins. "Okay, then," she says to Uncle Carl. "Be off with you. And close your mouth, Stanley Slater. What horrible manners! But not to worry, we'll work on that when I come to live with you in May." She blows a kiss to Mama. "Have my room ready, dear."

She's evil.

99.9 percent.

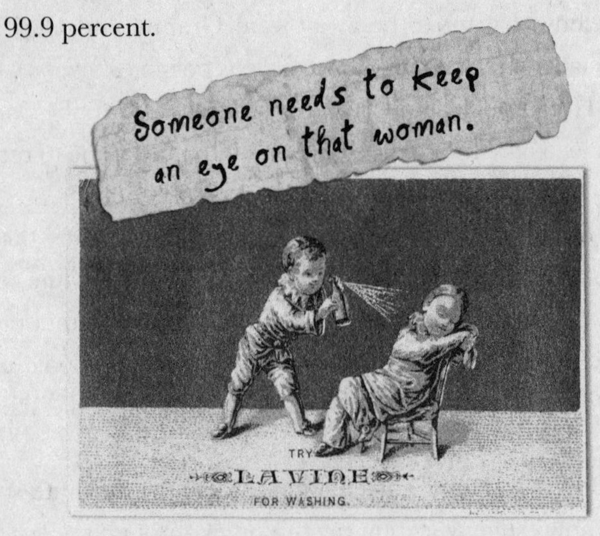

AUTHOR'S NOTE

In 1895, words were different, underwear was different, and diseases and their cures were different. So I had to do research. Lots and lots of research. And now I'm going to share those sources with lucky you!

LANGUAGE

Back in the 1880s, you wouldn't say something was "awesome." No, you'd say it was a "corker." If you got in trouble, you were "in the soup." If you cheated someone, you "skunked" her. If things went all "higgledy-piggledy," it wasn't necessarily a good thing. And if you spent the winter at a lumber camp, there were plenty of confusing terms you needed to learn. How do I know? Well, I used some of these resources.

A short list of slang words used in the nineteenth century, much to the chagrin of language snobs:

Nordquist, Richard, "The Triumph of Slang: Bosh, Humbug, and the Survival of 19th-Century Barbarisms," About.com Grammar & Composition, grammar.about.com/od/words/a/The-Triumph-Of-Slang.htm

As with any occupation, lumberjacks employed their own lingo, which varied from camp to camp. This is one list of terms, with a recording of the song "The Old Piney Woods."

"Lumber Jack & Pioneer Terms," Curtisville History & Pioneer Genealogies, curtisvillehistory.com/html/lumber_jack___pioneer_terms .html (last modified April 4, 2011)

A fun site where, among other things, you can plug in dates and see when certain American slang words began to be commonly used. Note that there's an option to search CLEAN or FULL. I highly recommend CLEAN.

"Historical Dictionary of American Slang," AlphaDictionary.com, alphadictionary.com/slang

Glossary of logging terms from the South Central Library System, and photographs and glossary from Wisconsin's past:

www.scls.lib.wi.us/mcm/rosholt/photos-from-wi-past/photoswi/images/00000013.pdf

LIFE IN THE LATE 1800S

McCutcheon, Marc. *The Writer's Guide to Everyday Life in the 1800s.* Cincinnati: Writer's Digest Books, 1993.

Schlereth, Thomas J. *Victorian America: Transformations in Everyday Life, 1876–1915.* New York: HarperCollins Publishers, 1991.

NAMES

A list of some eighteenth- and nineteenth-century American nicknames from the Connecticut state library:

ctstatelibrary.org/node/2329

Victorian-era names:

freepages.genealogy.rootsweb.ancestry.com/~poindexterfamily/OldNames.html

MEDICAL INFORMATION

This information from the Trail End State Historic Site in Sheridan, Wyoming, makes you wonder how anyone survived childhood in the late 1880s and early 1900s:

trailend.org/you-dangers.htm

Let's just say medicine has come a long way since the nineteenth century:

rootsweb.ancestry.com/~memigrat/diseases.html

Tomes, Nancy, PhD. "Public Health Then and Now: The Making of a Germ Panic, Then and Now." *American Journal of Public Health.* ajph.aphapublications.org/doi/pdf/10.2105/AJPH.90.2.191

WOMEN'S RIGHTS

Geri's interest in women's rights led to research on suffrage:

Eleanor Roosevelt: Battle for Suffrage (WGBH *American Experience*, PBS) pbs.org/wgbh/americanexperience/features/general-article/eleanor-suffrage/

"Women's Roles in the Late 19th Century," Conner Prairie Interactive History Park, connerprairie.org/Learn-And-Do/Indiana-History/America-1860-1900/Lives-Of-Women.aspx

DAY-TO-DAY NEWS AND EVENTS

"1890s Family," Federal Reserve Bank of Boston, New England Economic Adventure, economicadventure.org/pdfs/ml1890.pdf

"Growing Up in Michigan, 1880–1895: School Days," Michigan Historical Museum: www.hal.state.mi.us/mhc/growingup/schooldays.html

LIFE IN A LUMBER CAMP

Karamanski, Theodore J. *Deep Woods Frontier: A History of Logging in Northern Michigan.* Detroit: Wayne State University Press, 1989.

"Manistique Is Setting for Last Big Drive," *Wisconsin Rapids Daily Tribune,* July 25, 1929, genealogytrails.com/mich/schoolcraft/logdrive.html

"The Wisconsin Logging Book, 1839–1939," McMillan Library, mcmillanlibrary.org/rosholt/wi-logging-book/wilogging/index.pdf

"Wisconsin Lumberjack Story," Library of Congress: American Memories, American Life Histories: Manuscripts from the Federal Writers' Project, 1936–1940

wcwcw.com/feature83.htm

loc.gov/resource/wpalh3.38160207

And there's way more at my website (alisondecamp.com)!

IMAGE CREDITS

Archive.org
64, 239 (bottom right)
Author's personal collection
1, 3, 5, 7, 8, 11, 12 (bottom), 17 (both), 24, 29 (top), 34, 37, 41 (left), 48, 49 (bottom), 60 (top), 74, 81, 88, 90 (bottom), 94 (top), 103 (both), 111, 129 (bottom), 131, 134 (bottom), 135, 136, 137, 144, 149, 152 (both), 153, 155, 156, 158, 168, 172, 174, 180, 182, 185, 195 (bottom), 199 (bottom), 200, 201, 203 (left), 208, 211, 215, 218 (all), 231, 232, 238, 239 (top and bottom left), 243, 247
Beinecke Rare Book and Manuscript Library, Yale University Library
116 (left)
Biodiversity Heritage Library
15
Boston Public Library (https://creativecommons.org/licenses/by/2.0/)
29 (bottom), 38 (bottom), 85, 100, 102, 141, 151, 154, 159, 161, 178, 196, 199 (top), 203 (right), 205, 207, 214, 225, 227 (bottom), 234 (top)
British Library
41 (right), 189
Collection of Tom Graham
86, 176, 227 (top)
General public domain
9 (top), 10, 12 (top), 14, 42, 43, 45, 51, 52 (bottom), 55, 59, 62, 66 (both), 68, 75, 78, 80 (top), 90 (top), 94 (bottom), 107, 110, 164, 169, 187, 206
The *Globe,* December 20, 1890
54
Grand Marais, Michigan, Historical Society
27
John Oxley Library, State Library of Queensland
9 (bottom)
Library of Congress
18, 22, 25, 33, 38 (top), 40, 46, 47, 49 (top), 50, 52 (top), 56, 60 (bottom), 61, 67, 69, 71, 73 (both), 82, 83, 84 (top), 92, 95, 97, 98 (both), 99, 104, 105, 108, 113, 114 (right), 116 (right), 118 (both), 121, 122, 126, 127, 128, 129 (top), 132, 134 (top), 138, 140, 143, 146 (both), 162, 166, 190 (both), 191, 193, 195 (top), 209, 212, 217, 221, 223, 224, 226, 229, 230, 234 (bottom), 235, 237, 241
National Archives
80 (bottom)
National Library of Medicine
6, 20, 84 (bottom)
Schoolcraft County Historical Society, Manistique, Michigan
77
Topley Studio, Library and Archives Canada
58

This is my great-grandmother Cora. Apparently she loved babies and cats, and my mother loved her. But I think she looks crabby. She made my grandmother Alice get married at fifteen, which is exactly what someone that crabby would do. At sixteen, Alice had my uncle Stan, but since his father didn't stay in the picture for long, Alice and Cora took the baby Stan to a lumber camp to work for the winter. Eventually Alice married my grandfather, Ray McLachlan. He was not stinky, but according to my sister who remembers him, he *was* twinkly. I never knew any of these people, but the lore handed down through my family contributed to this story of Stan.

Guess who else kept a scrapbook? My great-grandmother. She filled it with ads and magazine covers and clippings from newspapers. I pored over it when I was young, I have it with me in my office now, and it inspired me to create Stan's book filled with quirky finds and comments.

Like Stan, I grew up in the Upper Peninsula of Michigan, where people say "Yah, eh?" and "Youse guys" and dress in many layers for seven months of the year. Unlike Stan, I had indoor plumbing and more than two pairs of pants. However, I might have worn the same sweater every day in fifth grade.

I'm the daughter of a hardware store owner (and reluctant occasional employee), and I spent too many school breaks attending Ace Hardware conventions and not enough at Disney World. After graduating from Michigan State University, I began teaching middle and high school English, where I dealt with students chewing tobacco during one of my amazing lessons, as well as a principal whose priority was fashion sense.

I admire teachers greatly.

After eight years, I quit teaching to stay at home with two babies who are now two teenagers. Babies and teenagers require almost the same amount of work. During this time, I taught myself to make glass beads and jewelry, which I sold at local galleries. When I'm not writing my next novel, I can occasionally be found "working" at Between the Covers bookstore in Harbor Springs or grocery shopping. My people like to eat.

For more information about *My Near-Death Adventures (99% True!)* and the author, visit alisondecamp.com.

Excerpt from

My Near-Death Adventures: I Almost Died. Again.

by Alison DeCamp

Published in the United States by Crown Books for Young Readers,
an imprint of Random House Children's Books,
a division of Penguin Random House LLC, New York.

CHAPTER 1

"What now, Stan? Huh? What do you want to do now?" Cuddy Carlisle's questions come at me like two hundred hungry mosquitoes buzzing around my head—they're hard to ignore and for some reason make me itchy.

"Do you have a rash?" Cuddy's eyebrows scrunch together as he peers up at me. "'Cause Mother says I am sensitive to rashes, Stan. I need to be careful."

I shake my head to reassure him. "No, no rash, Cuddy." Although just the mention of rashes and my skin starts tingling.

"Whew! That was a close one, wasn't it, Stan?" Cuddy chuckles before thankfully switching the topic. "Can we go to your house? Can I see that scrapbook of yours? Remember? You promised!"

It's true. I did. He was with me when I got the mail the other day. In it was a package from my good friend Stinky Pete.

He's a lumberjack, not a pirate.

Anyway, Stinky Pete sent me what is now my Most Prized Possession. My very own Mark Twain Self-Pasting Scrapbook. It's so fancy, it doesn't even need paste! Unfortunately, I told Cuddy he could see my scrapbook someday, and now I haven't heard the end of it. In fact, I haven't heard the end of a lot of things, like all three verses of "After the Ball," plus the verse that goes:

After the ball was over,
Bonnie took out her glass eye,
Put her false teeth in the water,
hung up her wig to dry,
Placed her false arm on the table,
laid her false leg on the chair,
After the party was over,
Bonnie was only half there!

Which was hilarious the first time I heard it, four years ago, and not the fifty-six times I've heard Cuddy bellow it in the last two days.

Why did I ever think it was a good idea to teach Cuddy that song in the first place? And why, oh, why did I have to run into Cuddy's mother while escaping from Mad Madge and her hooligan cousin Nincompoop?

Yes, Mad Madge is a girl. But she's unlike any other eleven-year-old girl I've ever seen. The only other person who comes close to her is my cousin Geri, and believe you me, that's not a good thing. Madge is mean and surly and uses words I've never heard before. Let's just say I'm highly suspicious of (a) her real age, and (2) her parents. I'm pretty sure one of them is a grizzly bear.

She is also fast. But not as fast as me. My heart was pumping as I zigzagged through the streets like a champ, making my getaway. I was as light-footed as a bare-knuckle boxer in the ring, and I was pretty sure Mad Madge couldn't catch me if she had wanted to.

Until, that is, I bumped into Mrs. Carlisle, a woman whose bones are so weak my slight nudge left her with a broken leg. That little accident also left me with the task of watching her son, Cuddy Carlisle, while she is on the mend and left my mama with the task of doing the Carlisles' laundry. For free.

"Also, Stan," Cuddy says, tugging on my sleeve, "if you didn't help watch me, Mother was going to have your mother pay for part of her medical bills, remember? Remember that part?"

There is no way Mama would be able to help pay anyone else's bills—we can barely pay our own. And when will I learn to keep my thoughts to myself instead of letting them flow through my lips like water from a well?

"I don't know when you'll learn that lesson, Stan," Cuddy says. His hands are red and sticky from the penny candy clenched in his pudgy fingers.

"C'mon, Cuddy," I sigh. "Let's go run those errands." I try to flatten the list Mrs. Carlisle gave me. It's long and will require at least four stops, which means Cuddy will talk to every single shop owner and customer and I won't get back to the boardinghouse to help Mama until all the boarders have eaten and all that's left for my growling stomach is a dry crust of bread and a pinch of salt.

"Here, Stan! You can have my candy!" Cuddy's hand juts into my face. The candy is covered with gullyfluff from his pocket and is glued to his hand like a sixth finger.

I'm no stranger to dirt or lint, but even I have my limits. "Um, no thanks, Cuddy," I say.

Kids.

"What did you say, Stan?" Cuddy runs to keep up with me.

I think quickly. I can't insult him. After all, I did make his mother an invalid. And even though he's only seven, calling him a kid can send him into a minor tantrum.

"Squids, Cuddy. I said 'squids.' "

"Why, Stan? Why were you talking about squids? Have you ever seen a squid? I know all about the giant squid! Do you want to hear about it?"

I shake my head no, but it doesn't matter. Cuddy is going to tell me about the giant squid anyway.

"Mother says my uncle Cuthbert—that's who I was named after—traveled all over the world and that's why I can't ever sit still. I'm just like him. So my uncle Cuthbert found a giant squid once in Newfoundland. Do you know where that is, Stan?"

He never waits for me to answer.

"It's in Canada, Stan. Do you know where Canada is, Stan? Huh? Do you?"

I nod and turn down the street toward the mercantile, gazing out over the milky, half-frozen bay, trains and ships steaming up the gray sky. I'm trying to keep both of Cuddy's feet on the boardwalk and out of the dirty, muddy road; Cuddy's grandmother doesn't appreciate a dirty Cuddy.

Mama says my accident with Mrs. Carlisle could have been worse—keeping an eye on Cuddy is a small price to pay. If we had had to help with Mrs. Carlisle's medical bills, we would have ended up in the poorhouse. Or if the weather were warmer, I'd be required to cart Cuddy's mom around on a Carrycycle like Jim McMaster does with his grandmother, Old Mrs. McMaster. Although everyone knows he only does that so she'll keep him in her will.

I look over Mrs. Carlisle's list:

1. Toilet soap
2. One tooth polisher
3. Cocoa
4. Baking powder
5. Shaving stick
6. Pick up order from Steinberg's

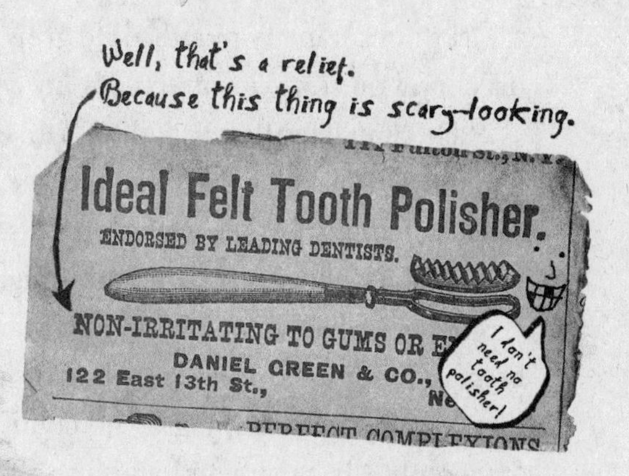

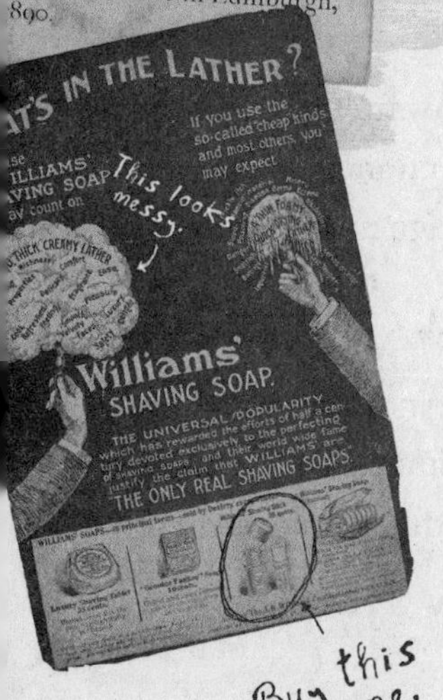

We're directly in front of Steinberg's so we dodge a couple of horses and slide in to pick up Mrs. Carlisle's order.

We pass shelves of cotton fabric stacked to the ceiling, some ready-made trousers and dresses, and thread displayed like candy behind glass counters. Cuddy picks up a vase full of buttons.

"Look, Stan! Look! I can balance this on my head!" I rush over just in time to catch the vase before it crashes to the floor.

"Nice catch, Stan!" He tries to clap but somehow his hands get stuck. I set the vase carefully down on the counter, hoping no one notices how sticky it is, and I realize his candy is gone.

"Cuddy," I say, grabbing both his shoulders, "where is your candy?"

"I thtuck it in my mouth." He grins and juice runs down his chin. I quickly wipe it up with my coat sleeve.

"Hi, Stan! Hey there, Cuddy!" Mr. Steinberg says. I push Cuddy and his sticky self behind me, praying he doesn't touch anything. "You picking up Mrs. Carlisle's order?" I nod. "I'll have that ready for you straightaway."

"Do you know anything about giant squids, Mr. Steinberg?" Cuddy asks, peeking around my back. "Did you know they eat children and dogs?" he continues without waiting for a reply. Mr. Steinberg hands me a brown paper package and laughs.

"No, Cuddy. Can't say as I was aware of that fact," he says before turning to answer the telephone.

"C'mon, Cuddy." I tuck the package under my arm and head for the door.

"Oh! Wait just a moment, boys!" Mr. Steinberg yells. "That was Mrs. Carlisle. She has one more item for you."

"The squid my uncle Cuthbert found was bigger than this store and had eyes the size of dinner plates," Cuddy says.

"She said not to bother wrapping it," Mr. Steinberg says as he takes a corset—a *corset*—off a nearby mannequin and hands it to me. "I'm afraid it's the last one and we want to make sure not to bend it, now, don't we?"

I am appalled. These people expect me to walk down State Street carrying a woman's undergarment like it's an everyday occurrence? Where is their sense of decency? What is this world coming to?

What if someone sees me?

"Here, Cuddy," I say, thrusting the corset into his hands. I had forgotten how dirty they were until he reached out. I think he has three flies and a dog stuck to them. I jerk the corset away. If he ruins it, I will probably have to replace it, and with all our money going to fix up the boardinghouse, Mama would certainly not understand if I had to buy some lady a new undergarment.

"C'mon, Cuddy," I say for the eleventh time since school got out. I snake my arm through the corset in an attempt to make it look like it's part of my coat, as if I have one very round, long sleeve. I try to convince myself no one will notice.

"That looks silly, Stan!" Cuddy yells from behind me. Three men turn around, and I feel my cheeks burn a path up to my ears. "You look like you have one giant arm. Like someone in the circus. Like a sideshow person. Have you ever gone to the circus, Stan? I have. I went to one in Chicago. There was a knife thrower and a tightrope walker and some trick monkeys. Mother wouldn't let me see the sideshows, but I saw a poster for a guy who could bend in half, and a teeny, tiny guy, and a lady with a beard. You look like you could be one of those people, Stan, don't you think? With that thing on your arm?"

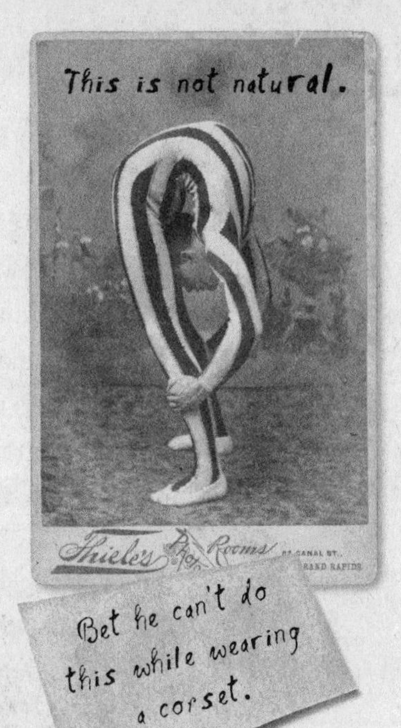

For a minute I think about bendy men and hairy ladies. I actually do want to know more, but it is not a good idea to encourage Cuddy's talking—one minute it's the circus, the next it's his grandmother's gout.

I learned that lesson the hard way.

"Should we go into Kreuger's, Stan?"

I just want to get this entire day over with. I want to drop off Cuddy and this dadgum corset. . . .

"Watch your mouth, Stan. You said 'dadgum,' and Mother always says that's a swear. I won't tell her you said a swear, but you might want to be careful, because Reverend Elliot says swearing's a sin. You shouldn't swear, Stan."

All I want to do is swear, but apparently even thinking of swearing can land me in a heap of trouble.

And then I see something up ahead that makes me stop in my tracks and want to utter every swearword I know.

"What in the blazes?" I mutter. I don't even care if Cuddy hears me.

"What was that? What did you say, Stan?" Cuddy stops next to me and catches the package from under my arm.

Carts fill the street, clopping down the semi-frozen ground, carrying goods and people through town. None of that is out of the ordinary.

"Did you see a giant squid, Stan?" Cuddy snorts and slaps his knee like he's told a great joke.

One wagon in particular has captured my attention like I'm looking through a camera and it's the only thing in focus.

It seems to speed toward us but takes a lifetime to get here. My ears feel full and my head swims. I recognize the driver, Uncle Carl, but he's not who I'm worried about. My breath catches as the wagon gets nearer. Is that who I think it is? A ramrod-straight spine. A nose so sharp it could cut glass. An old lady so mean I'm pretty sure even Vlad the Impaler would quake in his boots.

Fortunately, I'm wise to that woman's tricks. I square my shoulders and prepare myself for battle.

But then I see the most frightening sight of all. Peeking out of the wagon, under a heap of blankets, is a mess of unruly curls.

"Stan! I'm hungry!" Cuddy says.

For once, I'm not.

The old lady might be scary, but the person attached to that messy head of hair is downright dangerous.

She's been trying to kill me for years.